50

SPACESHIP TITANIC

SPACESHIP
TITANIC

RICHARD DUPREY
and
BRIAN O'LEARY

DODD, MEAD & COMPANY

NEW YORK

Published by Dodd, Mead & Company, Inc.
79 Madison Avenue, New York, N.Y. 10016
Distributed in Canada by
McClelland and Stewart Limited, Toronto
Manufactured in the United States of America
Designed by Nancy Dale Muldoon
First Edition

Library of Congress Cataloging in Publication Data

Duprey, Richard.
    Spaceship Titanic.

    I. O'Leary, Brian, 1940–   . II. Title.
PS3554.U57S6   1983   813'.54   83–11591
ISBN 0–396–08187–8

DEDICATED TO
THE BRAVE VOYAGERS
OF
THE AMERICAN AND SOVIET
SPACE PROGRAMS
WHO DIED
TO
FURTHER EXTEND MANKIND
OUT TOWARD
THE CHALLENGING STARS

Special thanks go to our literary agent,
Bill Reiss, who suggested the project
and brought the two of us together.

1

T MINUS two-hundred-eighty-eight minutes and counting translated to 0312 hours.

"Just spotted 'em between us and the viewing stand!" warned the young security guard in a whisper. His .38 was clear of its holster, in his hand. The other hand grasped the windscreen of the jeep.

"Which way?" demanded the driver.

"They're runnin' east, toward the launch pads."

The kid was sweating—back, neck, palms. It was more than Florida heat.

The figures they stalked were for an instant backlit by the lights on the bunting-draped grandstand and the Press Center.

The jeep ran in soft sand parallel with the runners' course. The sand muffled the sound of its tires.

"You watch 'em and I'll go where you say," suggested the driver. "Be careful with that gun!"

"Work in closer once they get out of the lights!"

"Got ya'."

It was a hell of a thing, unexpected. But then, he asked himself, why'd you take the job if you didn't want this?

"Can't the techs see 'em?" he asked.

Even though the jeep was gaining, it was amazing how quickly the intruders moved across the rough, scrubby reservation.

It wasn't as though the Space Center were deserted. There were techs, carpenters, painters, a whole galaxy of tradesmen swarming all over.

"We gainin' on 'em?" asked the driver.

"Take a looping left around that scrub ahead and we'll nail 'em on the hardtop."

The kid was excited. It was like a TV thriller. Only this was real. Clinging to the lurching, unsteady jeep, he had no idea what they'd stumbled on, but there was no way strangers should be running loose at the Cape five hours before a launch. Technological spies, vandals, Russians, whoever—you don't screw around with NASA.

The security jeep swung wide around a heavy copse of brush on high ground, then broke clear fifty yards ahead of the running figures on hard-packed dirt. The driver steered directly at the intruders.

"Dismount!" barked the driver as he braked hard, blocking the path of the oncoming runners.

The kid hit the dirt at a sprint and, as he held his balance, he whipped the Smith and Wesson forward into firing position, assumed his crouch, and yelled a warning.

"Freeze!" he ordered.

"Hands in the air!" yelled his partner, also clear of the jeep.

The runners halted, but neither reached.

"I said freeze!" the young guard shouted again. He was having trouble keeping his weapon steady.

What happened next took both guards unaware.

There came the cocking click of metal from the brush and a new voice, a deep one neither recognized, called out from somewhere behind them.

"*You* freeze! Drop those pieces! *Now!*"

"Who the—"

"*Drop them!*"

The kid opened his hand and let the pistol go. He heard his partner's weapon drop as well.

Two new sweat-suited figures stood beside them. Both had armaments leveled.

"Wh . . . what . . . the hell you people doin' here?" the kid managed. His voice was shaky, but he got it out. "You're on . . . on government property."

"And who you think you're drawing on?" challenged the man with the deep voice. He had a submachine gun leveled at the young guard's gut.

"Th . . . the . . . trespassers," he responded, pointing at the two runners who were drawing cautiously closer.

The moment was still tense. The silence was ominous.

"Hey, I'm sorry about this," said the leading runner in a friendly tone of voice. It was too dark out there to see his face. "My name's Leon Gill, staying on the base. I thought we'd cleared our running with your boss."

"*Gill?* Senator Gill?"

"That's right."

"Who are these guys?" asked the driver.

"My shadows."

"Secret Service," volunteered a man to the rear. He also held a folding submachine gun.

"You're Leon Gill?" asked the kid, amazed.

"Affirmative," said the man again. Then, turning his attention to his watchdogs, sounding very much the Marine Colonel he'd one time been, he ordered, "Let's put up the hardware and get on with our tour."

As quickly as it had begun the hunt was concluded, the confrontation defused.

The security guard felt like an ass. He'd just drawn on one of NASA's living legends, the man who'd likely be next Vice President of the United States.

"Cool, Senator," commented Ben Polikov, moments later, as they jogged closer to the launch pads. "You didn't turn a hair!"

"Runnin' out of hair," Gill called back over his shoulder.

"Just the same."

"They pay for coolness here," the Senator said, stopping again in deference to his younger companion who was puffing like a train.

The old pilot-astronaut seemed barely winded. He and his novelist companion had just run ten miles and had nearly been shot or at least arrested.

Both stood in sodden running clothes looking toward *Titan,* its immense form floodlit on Pad 39A.

"That's a far cry from the GI cans they expected us to fly back in the Mercury Program," Gill volunteered without taking his eyes from the incredible bird that stood balanced on its tail several thousand yards from where they'd paused.

The size of a McDonnell Douglas DC-9 airframe, the poised shuttlecraft looked like an almost triangular, overscale fighter plane strapped hard against a giant, cone-tipped fuel tank. Two more cylinders seemed to be lashed to the main tank's sides. The whole assembly, snow white, looked like a space-age replica of India's Taj Mahal, or like the main altarpiece for some strange new faith, an object to elicit awe and worship from the masses.

4

"What a fabulous feeling it'd be to fly that bird!" Gill spoke again. "The ultimate high!"

Even at sixty-six he was as spry as a man half his age. His motto, "Slow living, moderate exercise, fast flying," seemed to have proven a successful formula for at least one ex-NASA astronaut. United States senator, wealthy, respected, recently chosen candidate for Vice President, Gill had made it big.

"The shuttle's the most beautiful thing man's ever made," the Senator went on, shaking his oversized, heavily freckled skull. Gill had long ago lost all but a narrow fringe of hair but he'd kept his trademark freckles. They were scattered generously across his bald pate like jimmies on a single scoop of peach ice cream.

"We've come a long way," Polikov agreed.

Gill chuckled. "That's the best phrase you can find—you supposed to be Jim Michener's successor in the writing game?"

"I'm not Neil Armstrong," Polikov cracked back. "Not a phrasemaker for all space seasons."

"Hell, if you *were* Neil," the Senator came back, "you'd never have dragged your butt out here to take even one small step for health and fitness. He was eager enough to leap around the moon. On earth, we couldn't even make him run."

"Not sure I blame him."

"Used to claim there were only so many ticks in the old ticker. Didn't want 'em to run out while he was jogging!"

If there was one thing you could readily hear from Leon, reflected Polikov, it was a caustic cheap shot now and then directed at those of his comrades who'd walked the lunar surface. Jealousy, even when it's bubbled on a back burner for nearly thirty years, can still devastate.

"Took lots of believing to get this far!" Gill said, a note of feeling showing through.

They had come light years, reflected the writer, pleased to hear Gill swerve away from pettiness. The prospects for space were good right now. NASA and the Air Force were both flying shuttles regularly, launches just weeks apart—a hundred missions in all. The shuttle, able to reach velocities of 18,000 miles per hour, had evolved to the safest, soundest, most thoroughly tested technological system in mankind's history.

Political and financial pressure had even convinced NASA and its contractors to build and sell Space Star Enterprises, a commercial outfit with a shuttle transport, the one on 39A. The shuttle's maiden passenger-bearing flight to earth orbit, 200 miles up, was a scant five hours away. With a borrowed NASA crew, a passenger module stuffed with paying riders, they were on the brink of something bold and glorious!

"A lot of that believing was yours, Senator."

"Guess you could say that," Gill agreed.

Polikov hadn't been around for most of it. Until recently he'd depended, like the rest of the public, on what he read in the papers. He hadn't been standing close when Gill's "Original Seven" had been hurled ready-or-not into orbit to catch *Sputnik* and Gagarin. He hadn't seen close up those frantic days, those frustrating, sometimes heartbreaking days when they'd burned up boosters on the pad and good men had died in pointless jet mishaps or been incinerated on the ground in senseless and terrible fires.

"In many ways, it's all gravy now," the Senator added, sounding almost sad about it. "No more chills and spills. I'm more nervous about my speech in four hours than about the flight."

"Twenty seconds ago you were talking about the 'ultimate high.'"

"I know."

"Don't you approve of progress?"

"Sure I do, Ben. Of course I do. Haven't I given the best part of my life to it?" He paused to wipe the sweat from his forehead with the back of his hand. "It's just that something's slipped away from it. The boosters are bigger. The systems are a damn sight more dependable. Maybe it's gotten too slick, too perfect, too mechanically flawless. Maybe," he went on, "we've wandered too far from the old notion of space heroes, 'the right stuff,' Jason and his glorious Golden Fleece."

As Polikov stared up at the thunderbolt he too was about to mount and ride, the new Monarch of the Heavens, he was also moved to wonder.

Is there anything in heaven or on earth, Pete Sager speculated, reclining on his bunk, dressed in ragged cutoffs, better designed to contrast with a spaceship than a classic, character sailboat? His boat rocked gently under him, responding to the unspoken question.

There is nothing, he conjectured onward, in the warm oil-lamp glow of his cabin, like a clunky, funky, wooden ketch to slow the hustling world to a crawl, to give a proper human being a chance to breathe.

"Aren't you coming?" Sara called from the forward cabin.

"Not at the moment!" Pete called back impishly.

"Wise ass!"

Sassafrass, all forty-seven feet of her, was tied to the NASA dock there on Indian River to the west of the reservation. It had taken a lot of negotiation and a lot of hell-raising to get the powers-that-be to permit Sager's

7

boat to "crap up the landscape," as one of the surly PR types shipped in from Houston chose to put it.

"Listen, Tim," Pete had shouted at Tim Oates, Space Star's Director of Operations. "You picked Jay Pepper as Command Pilot and got me to play second banana to NASA's champion asshole. You offered me half the pay the flight is worth. You installed Pepper in a damn cottage where he can screw himself crosseyed with the local talent, then you bitch at giving me a few feet of dock space to tie my boat!"

"You could have had a cottage, Peter. I told you that!" Oates was sweating.

"I live on a damn boat. You know that. I don't belong in a candy-ass cottage!"

Maybe that was it, Pete reflected. Maybe that's why Astronaut Peter Sager was always a bridesmaid, never a bride. Throughout the whole space shuttle program Pete was always stuck in the right-hand seat.

"If you're not coming in here," Sara called insistently, interrupting his meditation, "I might as well put on my clothes and chase back to Orlando."

Maybe that was why, he kept on considering, refusing to be distracted by the mating call of his latest lady, even the big rollers, the money boys who'd been given development rights to the shuttle, seemed unwilling to give him command. He was the outsider, the loner, the one "exotic" remaining in a stable of neatly barbered, clean-cut pilot-astronauts. The man who lived on vintage sailboats, shaved only when on duty, and who'd been involved in very public and very messy divorces was not the sort to inspire confidence with a pressurized cabin full of fatcats paying incredible quantities of coin of the realm for the privilege of taking a couple of quick spins around the globe.

"Peter, for Christ's sake. You have to leave in less than an hour."

"What the hell!" he said to himself. Maybe a little action on the Vee-berth would psyche him up for the shuttle flight. It might compensate him in advance for a dull day of flying copilot to Jay Pepper.

He wriggled out of his cutoffs.

"I am entering descent mode, Houston," he called out cheerfully. "Shuttlecraft is about to initiate full docking procedures forward!"

She giggled. "It's about time," she called out.

If there was one infallible way to turn on a genuine space groupie—even the young wife of one of Orlando's most prominent proctologists—it was to talk to her in terms of "docking procedures." It seemed to get 'em every time!

Launch Control was cranking up to a higher pitch of activity as the countdown proceeded.

There was a disturbance by the launch director's desk.

"What the hell's going on?" barked a perspiration-drenched, agitated Tim Oates.

Launch Director Karl Heinz looked up startled from some outdated weather maps before him. "Other than a countdown, I'll be damned if I know." As always, Karl sounded calm.

"But what's this about another screwup with your computers?" There were beads of sweat popping out all over Oates's ruddy forehead.

"This place is a rumor factory," Heinz responded. "Don't believe all you hear."

"Do we have a problem?"

"No."

"You're sure?"

9

"Yes."

At that point, Oates began to deflate. Heinz could see it happen.

It was a fascinating phenomenon, thought the stubby German. So many times he'd watched the slender, patrician Oates swell up, turn scarlet, and begin perspiring like a plough-horse. It was an incredible physical metamorphosis. The biology involved would be incredible!

"The countdown is right on schedule, Mister Oates." He indicated the countdown clock with a gesture. "Fueling goes fine. Onboard computers go fine. Communications are nominal. All you have to do is put your crew aboard, hook them up, insert passengers in the proper places, and I'll give you a sweet honey of a launch." He kissed his fingers like a Frenchman.

If Heinz sounded smug it was because he'd become utterly confident. Even though Space Star had assumed responsibility for passenger flights and for some of the other commercial ventures now occupying part of the overall space effort, hands-on implementation was still for the most part with NASA and its primary contractors. Karl Heinz himself had already presided over thirty-eight of the hundred shuttle launches to date and had been scrubbed only twice, a record, he was confident, that would stand up for a considerable period of time to come.

"Well, that sounds a little better."

"So don't believe all the rumors you hear," warned the veteran launch director, trying to underscore the lesson he hoped Oates had just picked up. "I take half of it with warm water and salt. For example, I even get a rumor today that your lottery was fixed."

"*My* lottery?"

"Space Star's."

10

"Where in the hell'd you hear that?"

"Some of my technicians. Some of the ground crew out there. Word has it that an extra quarter-million dollars would buy a place on this flight. Scalping, I think it's called here. Does that sound about right?"

"That's bullshit!" Oates snapped, threatening to balloon back up again. "The lottery was strictly on the up-and-up. Didn't matter who you were. If we drew your number, you got to buy a ticket. I'll stake my ass on it!"

Heinz's eyes crinkled at the corners behind his thick glasses. "Sure anyone would want it?" he asked.

Before Oates could think of an appropriate rejoinder, someone placed a new report in front of Launch Director Heinz.

"Better look at this, Karl," said the message bearer gravely.

"Uh!" Heinz grunted as he scanned the new data on the desk in front of him.

"What the hell's gone wrong now?" demanded a very jumpy Oates.

"Look here," said Heinz, sounding every bit as calm as he had been before. "Look at this weather map." Marking with a soft pencil, he showed Space Star's overall operations chief the latest weather outlook for the region. "There's a line of crap moving this way— thunder squalls. If the wind stays the same, we got maybe twenty minutes to play with at launch time. If it picks up some ground-speed, we get a first-class boomer at launch and maybe we get an acid shower for the crowd."

"Damn it all to hell!" exploded Oates. His face reddened and the sweat appeared almost on cue. "What do we do?"

11

"Simple," said Heinz. "We stay on time."

"Do you think we can?"

The little gnome grinned.

"I do *my* part, Timothy. I do mine. My launch crew does theirs. Just keep after them tiny folk you got watching out over the passenger roster. We don't get nobody running for the train at the last second, okay? You fill up the coach on time, I blast it off on time. It's a deal?"

For a moment, Oates just stared.

Finally, he responded. "Deal, Karl. It's a deal!"

The countdown clock showed T minus two-hundred-fifty-six.

A whole sequence of neon lights blinked systematically on and off in front of Cocoa Beach's Liftoff Motel. First, the letters L I F T O F F came on in brilliant green. The rocket itself was next, marked off in blue tubing. Then a halo of fire around the base of the rocket was struck in strident red. Finally the whole garish business was illuminated at once, including the white tubing swirls designating smoke. After a full second's life, the whole business flicked off to repeat the sequence.

In the drab room the owners designated The Saturn Suite, voices could be heard murmuring in flawless Letzburgesch, a dialect of German.

"You're not asleep," the male voice said aloud.

"A question or a statement?" the female voice asked.

"Does it matter?"

"Not now it doesn't," she replied with the classic heavy sigh. "I'm wide awake."

"Don't try to convince me you were asleep," he said, shifting his position for at least the hundredth time.

"I wasn't," she admitted. "How could I be? This place is a veritable pest-hole."

"A dungeon."

"Our family has slept in dungeons before," she noted. "Haven't I ever told you about Willi the Bold?"

He laughed out loud.

"Of course," she added quickly. "There have been a good many members of my family who deserved to *rot* in their dungeons."

Princess Constance of Luxembourg and Prince Conrad, her consort, may not have qualified as major league royalty by some standards, but the bloodlines were legitimate. Considering the status of international royalty in the late eighties, Space Star's PR staff had done well to get any truly blue blood to mix with the more conventional red blood and green money of the lottery-chosen cash customers.

"Maybe we should have asked them to meet the plane in Miami instead of renting the station wagon," said Prince Conrad. "At least they might have put us in a first-class hotel instead of this . . . this . . . sack of fleas."

"Nonsense," answered the Princess. "You know how I detest fawning little men with carnations in their buttonholes!"

With that, they terminated their brief conversation and tried to get back to sleep. The neon lights blinked on and off outside, but after a while both managed to doze off. There is, after all, some truth in the legend that the true aristocrat does well under stress.

The viewing grandstand stood three miles west of the launch pad. Decked out with festive awnings and the obligatory red, white, and blue bunting, swagged with American flags, it proudly awaited the crowd.

The scene was beginning to come alive.

Space Star Enterprises had set up both Press Center

13

and Passenger Departure Gate near the viewing grand-stand. The thinking was that centralizing all of the principal non-launch operations in a single, highly visible locale would make it much more convenient for media coverage, enhancing the likelihood that the world at large wouldn't miss a single beat of their incredible space bash. Following the policy of NASA before them, Space Star believed in a wide-open public relations stance, one that would keep the public fully informed of what was happening, even while it was happening. That was, as David Locke, Space Star's President, was frequently quoted as saying, "The American, free-market way to do business!"

Although the press buses were only now beginning to disgorge the advance guard of cameramen and technicians, along with a scattering of on-the-air broadcasters representing American and foreign radio and TV networks, an army of people had already toiled through the night—carpenters, electricians, painters, security personnel.

From the very first moment the fifty fortunate space travelers had been notified of their selection by lottery for the maiden flight, during their short, near-home training programs, their physical examinations, and the excited weeks of bragging and butterflies, the emphasis had been on careful coordination. Americans had learned throughout their brief but intensive history of space flight that such is inevitably the key to success.

"You got your passengers pinned down?" Tim Oates asked a harried Ted Bassano, Space Star's Director of Public Relations, who was personally going over the passenger list while standing by the departure gate in wrinkled slacks and a now sweat-soaked short-sleeve sports shirt.

14

"All my tourist-class gang will be picked up from their lodgings by 0600 hours local time. I've surveyed motels, residences, lodgings and they're all in place. They'll be ushered past this gate on their way to the pad at 0630 so the TV cameras can get a peek at them. They'll be bused then to 39A so they can board by 0700 or T minus sixty as it translates currently."

Ted was officious but there was no question he was doing a superior job.

"What about first-class passengers, our million-dollar babies?"

Bassano peered down at the typed list on the clipboard through the ridiculous half-moon glasses he wore for reading. Oates, a holdover from NASA, had scant use for anyone who needed glasses. Weakness was weakness, no matter how one tried to disguise or compensate for it.

"Senator Gill's been jogging all over the Cape during the night, driving Bob Murchison's security people out of their minds. He's got that Jewish novelist guy with him. My Arab prince is coming in from Orlando by chopper. He brought his own. The Speaker of the House is over at Patrick Air Force Base with his wife. They'll come over by chopper too, with the couple from Dallas. Our movie stars are on the base as are Mister Locke and his bride."

Oates gave Bassano a look. It had been a while since anyone might have described Essie Locke as a bride.

"Garson's yacht was spotted by the Coast Guard twenty minutes ago on Indian River. He's almost bang on schedule and . . . and . . ." As he stared down at the clipboard, his knuckles whitened and all the color seemed to drain out of his swarthy face.

"Susie!" he called out. "*Susie!*"

Oates had never seen an Italian so pale.

"What's the matter?" he demanded.

"Susie, I need you!" Bassano was howling now, looking everywhere for his assistant, Susie Pitcairn. "Susie, where the hell are you?"

"Bassano, what's got into you?"

"My princess!" the little man shouted.

"What?"

"Princess Constance. The Princess of Luxembourg. I don't know where they put my princess!"

With that, the almost frantic bantam rooster was gone, charging off across the open field toward the viewing grandstand, shouting for Susie.

But Tim Oates had neither time nor excess energy to chase after him. He had to get together with his launch director to go over the latest radar reports on that line of squalls already approaching Orlando. Bassano and Susie Pitcairn would have to find their own princess. He had a bird to launch.

He was a competent yacht skipper, holding the appropriate Coast Guard ticket and a fair amount of experience, but *String of Pearls* was new to him and a hell of a lot of boat.

"There's your last red blinker, Cap'n," called out Garson's pimple-faced nephew who had, in his zeal to be helpful, turned out to be a first-class pain-in-the-ass.

"Thanks, kid. I got it!"

Actually, the channel down the Indian River from New Smyrna hadn't been too bad, if you didn't run into an island in the dark. He had done his homework, going over the Coastal Pilot, all but memorizing the appropriate entries in the *Cruising Guide to the Southern Coast*, and studying the right charts. At least that phase of the voyage had gone right.

Overall, however, the sprint down the Atlantic coast from Block Island Sound had been a near disaster. It was one thing to move a boat—even with the owners aboard—and another thing altogether to have to stick to a schedule as undeviating as the one old man Garson had given him.

"Do you understand, Laurence?" Garson had repeated over and over when they talked about the plan in Newport. "We can't afford to be more than a half-hour late or I'm out two million dollars."

Two million dollars, the young skipper reflected, was a hell of a lot of money even with inflation. As a professional boat bum, would he ever see that much money cross his palm in a whole lifetime? He doubted it. Two million dollars for a day in space! What a wacky world!

"I'll get you there in time, sir," he'd blandly assured the old fart. "Don't you worry none about that. I ain't never let an owner down yet. My references should tell you that."

But the assurance that he'd keep things on a space-age schedule had been delivered before the radar pooped out, before the starboard engine developed a chronic case of the overheats, before they nearly got slammed off Hatteras, and before he discovered what a gold-plated bitch Betsey Garson was. All the little tramp wanted to do was catch him in the chart room or to talk raunchy at him on the bridge. It raised hell with his concentration.

"How can they drink cocktails in space?" demanded the snot-nosed nephew again. He'd been asking the question all night. The skipper should have sent the little turd below hours ago and gotten a real crewman up there on the bridge with him.

"Huh? How?" the kid persisted.

The skipper improvised. "I've heard they serve 'em with a special kind of straw and a crushable plastic can. Yeah," he went on, pleased by his own inventiveness. "They pour the booze into a plastic can with a thing halfway between a straw and a nozzle sticking up out of it. Then, while they're all bumpin' around up near the ceiling all friendly and weightless, they spray the drinks down their throats. They don't even have to swallow."

The kid's acne-scarred face got even redder than before. The man could see it even in the dim light on the bridge.

"I don't need you makin' fun of me!" the kid snarled. With that, he stormed off below, leaving the captain in solitary possession of the bridge just as he was about to make his final approach to the NASA dock.

"Let's have a couple of you deck apes topside to take lines," he ordered over the intercom system. "Hop to it!"

No sooner had he spoken than two figures appeared on deck. That was one good thing about working for an autocrat like Garson. People moved.

It was then he spotted the ketch tied to the dock ahead. He shook his head in wonderment. It looked like a pirate ship berthed at a spaceport.

Likely it was nothing but a cold. Young children often signal the start of a routine respiratory infection with a high temperature.

The timing had been so incredibly bad. It was T minus two-hundred-thirty-one. In less than an hour Mrs. Crabtree would pull into the carport in her Beetle.

Judy Langenberg, as she'd chosen to be called again, could already hear the fuss the old woman would make.

"You're leavin' me with a sick chile?" Ella would ask with exaggerated disbelief, shaking her head and putting her large, ebony hands on what Judy felt sure were the widest hips on the North American continent.

"Don't that beat all?" the woman would continue, shaking her head dolefully. "Dis chile's burnin' up with the fever and her maw goes spinnin' roun' the whole world with a bunch of fancy folk!"

"But it's my job, Ella," she'd come back, defending herself, her maternal concern.

Ella'd continue to shake her head and cluck like a disapproving hen until Judy left for the launch.

"And I'll be home tonight!"

It was incredible, Judy thought, sitting there in her pajamas next to her own bed where she'd earlier moved Karen. To circumnavigate the globe twice before breakfast and lunch. To take off from Florida in the morning, to land in California early afternoon after two complete orbits, and then to jet back to Florida in time to kiss her daughter goodnight. It was mind-boggling!

But you've trained for it, she told herself simply and directly. You're overtrained for it, as a matter of fact. "Astronaut–Payload Specialist," they called her. It was an imposing title and it involved a tremendously demanding course of training. From the incredible physical and psychological evaluation of five years back, the thousands of boring lectures in Houston, the jet flight training and the physical conditioning, to say nothing of eleven shuttle flights, it had been quite a career. Had it all been worth it, however, to serve cocktails and soothe frightened multimillionaires in a weightless cabin two hundred miles up?

19

She could hear Karen's regular, rhythmic breathing. The flush on her lovely young face seemed to have receded. She appeared to be sleeping well. Judy leaned forward and lightly brushed the child's forehead with the palm of her hand. She was careful not to startle her, to awaken her.

The child seemed markedly cooler.

There was only one part of the mission scheduled for 0800 hours that Judy really deplored. It was actually a stupid coincidence. It was no one's fault. But it was, nonetheless, an embarrassment, something she wasn't really prepared to handle. As part of the show, they were scheduled to rendezvous with *Spacelab VII*, the European Space Agency's entry into the space stampede.

On first examination such an operation would be routine. No crew or passenger exchange was planned. *Titan* would merely maneuver past. There'd be waving and an exchange of radio messages, and the passengers would get a complete rundown on the European vehicle and its crew. Then the two ships would break off visual contact and would go their respective ways.

The one catch was that Ian Stafford, British astronaut trained on a special exchange by NASA in Houston, served as command pilot of *Spacelab VII*. Until eight months ago, Ian had been Judy Langenberg's husband.

The current ripped through as the skipper eased *String of Pearls* closer to the dock. The strange ketch named *Sassafrass* was tied securely and professionally, but the man at the big power yacht's helm wasn't pleased with its placement. It took too much room.

"Goin' in?" called one of the deck apes, holding a line up forward, ready to loop it over a piling.

"One more pass," the skipper said, frankly disgusted

with himself. Maybe if he came around again he could let that fickle current swing him in like closing a gate.

The red light came on again indicating the starboard engine was overheating.

"Damn!"

Not enough trouble!

Pete Sager was totally distracted. Sara, beneath him, was putting on a spirited if somewhat noisy demonstration.

"Go, Peter, go!" she moaned, rolling her blond head back and forth. "Go! Go! More, for God's sake! Harder!"

What did the insatiable woman want?

Never one to say "die," Pete toiled manfully to oblige the lady. A little more bounce and he'd brain himself on the overhead.

And it was precisely because of the ever building rhythm of their violent lovemaking, punctuated by her enthusiastic groans, that Pete, normally the alert and almost intuitive sailor, failed to hear the gutteral, muted vibrations of the brawny power yacht struggling to settle in next to them.

As a matter of fact, the sweaty, passionate scene in the Vee-berth was just achieving its shuddering crescendo when the big craft from Newport, catching more current suddenly than its skipper anticipated, swung into *Sassafrass* with a vigorous jolt.

"Yes!" Sara cried out exultantly, urging more such Herculean efforts. "Oh, yes!"

But suddenly and mysteriously her lover was gone, abruptly flown from her embrace.

A furious, utterly naked sailboat skipper stood on deck as the eastern sky began to brighten, shaking his fist wildly at a floating apartment house that had just swung into him.

"You all right?" the power boat's skipper shouted down.

"No thanks to you!"

"The current caught me."

"Today, I'm flyin' a frickin' spacecraft and you, jackass, can't even lay a stinkpot against a pier!" Pete Sager shouted at the idiot hanging over the rail above him.

"What's that?"

Pete was about to repeat it when he saw the headlights of the vehicle coming to get him.

"Oh, to hell with it," he said. It was time to throw on some clothes and get to the launch.

It was obvious *Sassafrass* had weathered the impact and he'd get no satisfaction wrangling with the liveried jokers of the big boat's crew.

As he slid down the companionway to find his clothes, Pete did have one jarring thought. My God, he said to himself, flinching even as the notion struck home. What if she thinks I can do that every time!

2

THE count stood at T minus one-hundred-eighty-seven minutes.

The sun still hadn't made an appearance. It seemed content to send a rosy glow ahead of it and was yet lying somewhere below the horizon.

Things were becoming hectic around the main gate. Cars, vans, trucks, buses were pouring aboard in a steady stream. One might have the distinct impression that half the United States was on the road that very morning, with a large number of them trying to crash the party at the Kennedy Space Center.

"Gonna' earn our bread today, babe!" called one of the civilian gate guards to the other. Both were fully occupied, standing a few feet apart, directing a double file of traffic onto the reservation.

"Beats just sittin'!"

"Amen to that!"

There was something exciting, stimulating, inspiring, even, about being part of the final preparations for a launch. There'd been too little going on in the seventies at the Cape. There were times when it seemed the country had excluded "space" and "rocket" from its vocabulary altogether. Until the blooming of the space shuttle program, personnel at Kennedy had become dispirited. Things seemed to slide and get lax. However, the space shuttle offensive, beginning with *Columbia* in '81, had the effect of turning things around.

"Lots of dollars in this crowd!"

"You know it!"

"Some of these cars are too much."

And so it went with the two guards exchanging observations, commentary, as they checked credentials and waved visitors aboard.

The weather was already sticky and damp. The atmosphere smelled as if it'd rain sometime before the eventful day had run its course. There were thunder showers in the region. That was, of course, one thing no one wanted—the possibility of rocket fuel residue and rain mixing to bring on a stinging, hydrochloric acid shower!

"Look what we got right here!" called the first guard.

Three buses sporting the device of the United States Marines approached the gate.

"They're gonna' roast off their buns in those red tunics."

"Who is?"

"Marine Band."

"How'd we get *them?*"

"Gill was a Marine."

"You're right. Forgot."

They waved the buses through.

"Seems like *his* show, doesn't it?"

"He got the package through the Senate."

"Nice he gets the first ride."

Abruptly, the first guard halted a black limo with a passenger tag stuck on its windshield. "Official *Titan*" shouted the tag in Day-Glo orange. There was nothing wrong, but the guard had promised he'd pull up this one car when it came. He owed it to himself.

"What's wrong, officer?" asked the driver, putting down the window, gesturing toward the numbered tag.

"Just spot-checkin'," said the guard, eyeballing the back seat passengers. "Nothin' wrong at all."

Sure enough, it was Missy Grace. The older lady was likely her mother or companion. The girl reminded him of the frightened doe he'd shot on his first hunting trip a hundred years ago. She wasn't anywhere near as glamorous in person as on TV, in the films. There were already sweat crescents under the arms of her pink blouse.

"Enjoy your jeans commercials on TV, Miss Grace," he called to her cordially.

It made him mad that the girl neither smiled nor reacted in any way at all.

"Keep movin'," he snapped at the puzzled driver.

The big car jolted swiftly forward.

"Who was that?" called the other man.

"Bigshot bitch!" he replied. He didn't feel like talking anymore.

"Hold up!" The second guard halted a dusty station wagon with a mountain of luggage piled in the back. It carried no identification to indicate it belonged at the Space Center.

"We're just a bit behind our schedule," said the driver with a heavy European accent.

"Have a pass of any kind, sir?"

"I can show you passports or our tickets for the flight."

A fortyish woman, strong-featured but good-looking in

25

a pleasant way, leaned over toward the window. "We're Princess Constance of Luxembourg and Prince Conrad. We're a little late, I think, for our ride in space."

The guard had a strong temptation to identify himself as a former President from up the line in Georgia, but he resisted.

Other than the accents, the couple in the wagon were like tourists from Milwaukee.

"Would you pull over there, sir, and stop your car?"

He took the passports, blocked his lane, and followed the wagon over on foot.

"Problem?" called his fellow guard.

"Nothin' I can't fix," he answered with a grin. "Got a prince and princess here." He rolled his eyes heaven-ward.

The two space pilots sat behind the outdoor table with the red felt top. They wore sparkling white flight suits with the blue and gold logo of Space Star on the breast. It was a blue five-pointed star surrounded by a pair of what looked like double quotation marks. The orange sun was beginning to come up behind them. It made a fine picture.

Ted Bassano was satisfied that TV lights bouncing from the crimson table top wouldn't make the two of them grisly gray the way green felt had done during his PR rehearsal days ago.

"At what altitude will you drop the two smaller tanks, Commander Pepper?" asked a reporter.

"At approximately forty kilometers," answered Astro-naut Pepper. "My passengers won't feel a thing." He smiled, the Perfect Astronaut, close-cropped, reddish blond hair in wavy rows glistening like wire.

"Where will they fall?"

26

"In the Atlantic Ocean from which they'll be recovered by barge for eventual reuse."

"What about the main tank?"

"Into the Indian Ocean forty minutes after launch."

"We note you're supposed to land at 0800 Pacific Time," broke in a girl reporter from the front row. "Why so short a flight?"

"Two orbits are sufficient to permit the earth to rotate enough beneath us to make a California landing with a minimum of maneuver, ma'am," responded the command pilot smoothly. "Works out as a very neat flight. Out at eight; in at eight." Then he smiled his intrepid young space hero smile. It wasn't for nothing his fellows in the service called him "Cap'n Cleancut."

"There's another reason we've kept the flight a little short," put in Astronaut Peter Sager, looking just a trifle worn. "There's gonna' be some folks aboard who'll get a little queasy from the weightless state. We all get a touch of it from time to time. We didn't want to . . . to prolong the agony, so to speak."

Ted Bassano, standing off to the side, groaned softly to the girl standing next to him. "That's all we need," he complained. "Why'd we have to pick this clown?"

The press conference would extend for a few more minutes. Then the flight crew would board a van to be hauled three miles east to the shuttle on 39A. As expected, Pepper had done them proud, speaking with his clear, confident baritone, the perfect image of their spaceflier's trade, an exemplary, lantern-jawed figure for the nation to watch on early morning TV, to identify with.

Sager'd been good, too, surprisingly so, interjecting little touches of humor here and there—nothing alarming or indiscreet except the crack about airsickness. De-

27

spite the chalky voice and the somewhat sarcastic image he created, he'd pulled no major boners.

"Why California?" a reporter asked.

Sager jumped in to answer. "The runway's a little short in Tahiti!"

There was a ripple of laughter.

"Cap'n Pepper," asked a middle-aged man with a messy madras jacket and a shock of iron gray hair. "Do you truly believe we've come to the point where space travel is as simple and as safe as getting on a scheduled airliner?"

"Simple, no," said Pepper. "Safe, absolutely. Other than the brief training protocol built into this particular program, the careful physical examinations, and the—"

"The price of the tickets," interrupted Sager.

Bassano groaned again.

"What I'm trying to say," Pepper insisted, recovering the floor, "is that for all practical purposes we're at that point in time right now. That's a safe, totally airworthy system out there. It's a proud day for all Americans. Our distinguished list of passengers, our brilliant guests on Space Star today, will be as safe as if they were at home watching the tube."

Bassano nearly burst his buttons. It was the perfect windup. He started the throat-cutting gesture to signal Pepper it was time to stop, time to capitalize on a masterful closing statement.

Pepper, however, had one more sentence to add.

"So we'll fly them home safe and sound tonight," he promised, flashing The Smile once more, "providing I don't push the wrong button."

Even Tim Oates, only half listening, blanched at that one in the Operations Blockhouse.

"Did you hear what that . . . that asshole said?"

28

"You picked him," said Launch Director Heinz, shaking his head.

Astronaut–Payload Specialist Judy Langenberg was the first of *Titan*'s flight crew to board. The schedule called for her thirty tourist-class passengers to be established in place before those upstairs in the higher-priced seats.

Titan's passenger module was fourteen feet in diameter and fifty feet in overall length. With two completely independent pressurization systems, the two passenger levels—first-class on the top, tourist below—were connected with each other and with *Titan*'s cockpit by an air lock.

Judy's people were to be boarded and secured in place by T minus sixty minutes. Some of them had already passed the viewing stand and were on their way by jitney to 39A. It was T minus one-hundred-twenty-four when she descended into the then perpendicular lower compartment to give it a check before admitting her flock.

The whole passenger compartment of the spacecraft was a marvel of ingenuity. It struck Judy every time she looked at it: people-oriented engineering carried to the ultimate. Incredible tilting seat-couches with a whole battery of safety locks and redundant watchdog devices; decor carefully devised by psychologists and bio-engineers to soothe nervous passengers, to put them in a receptive frame of mind for the wonders to which they'd be exposed.

Passenger observation of liftoff and reentry would be limited to closed-circuit television viewing over one of the big screens in the front of each passenger level. Once *Titan* was established in orbit, however, the complete passenger module, like a great cylindrical tank, would be eased up and out of the cargo bay by means of an automatic crane so the passengers could see from the specially designed windows, airline-type ports in tourist, "vista dome" arrangements for first class.

"It's all set up for you, ma'am," called one of the contractor's technicians as Judy climbed aboard to assume her duties.

"Thanks, Jimmy," she acknowledged.

"Hope you have a sensational flight, ma'am," he added with a shy smile as he left her brightly lit section of the spacecraft. *Why* did he persist in calling her ma'am? She despised it.

Judy, a qualified astronaut in contrast to Ron Fisher, an airline steward from Pan Am chosen for the other billet, had been first proposed to preside in *Titan*'s first-class section where the level of creature comfort and posh mechanical innovation was far beyond anything ever attempted in an air transport system. Seniority and training entitled her. But Judy turned it down. The sybaritic splendor of it, with fully reclining couches on deck under observation domes, turned her off. That, coupled with the weightless cocktail lounge, gave everything the feeling of a decadent Roman banquet. All that splendor was more than the daughter of a commercial pilot from Northfield, Minnesota, should have to deal with. Judy felt that her personality and background better suited the needs of the tourist-class passengers, despite the fact that on this inaugural flight even they had paid two hundred thousand dollars each for the privilege of tagging along.

Everything was in order. But to herself she groaned a little at the prospect of all that had to be accomplished in the next sixty minutes. Thirty people, who had been subjected to a modest training program of approximately

30

fifty hours—mainly theoretical "book" training—had to climb down a perpendicular ladder into the spacecraft, have their various fears and phobias patiently attended to, be secured safely and comfortably to their seats, and then be dealt with cheerfully and constructively for an hour or more of final countdown. All of this to be accomplished by one rather weary young woman.

For a moment her mind turned back to Karen. She wondered whether the child would feel well enough to watch the launch on TV or whether Ella Crabtree would allow her up to do so.

"Anything wrong, ma'am?" asked the last of the technicians, noting the troubled look on her face as he passed her on the ladder.

"Uh-uh," she assured him, continuing with her checkout of the disposition of the cabin. "And *don't*," she added with mock fierceness, "call me *ma'am!*"

They rode one of the NASA vans that had been repainted with Space Star's logo. They drove swiftly toward the launch pad.

"Somebody's got to fetch me that book," insisted Commander Pilot Pepper. The Pepper jaw was jutting and there was a certain edge to the Pepper voice, a note of rebuke in the way he made his demand known, that suggested *he* was somehow the aggrieved party. Someone else was at fault and it was surely someone else's responsibility to rectify the situation.

"How important is it, Commander?" asked the man designated to be Oates's second assistant. "This book."

"It's his flight log," Sager put in.

The Space Star man was a flunky for all his titular magnificence.

"It's not important," said Pepper. "It's critical."

Pete Sager didn't know whether to laugh aloud or vomit with disgust. There was no denying that Pepper was a decent space pilot. He'd been an outstanding jet-jockey in the Navy and, like all of the men still with the Agency, he knew his business well. But for all his piloting ability, for all his flawless public image, for all the PR-puff, Pepper was a tough human being to take, self-absorbed, demanding beyond reason, defensive with peers, and belligerent and condescending with those he thought he could bamboozle. He'd been that way in the Navy, too.

"You are sure where you left it, aren't you?" Oates's man asked him one more time.

"I *do* know where it is," Pepper came back, wriggling away from acknowledging again that *he'd* left the log book anywhere. "Affirmative!"

"And where is that, one more time?"

"Table. Front room. Shall I draw you a diagram?"

"Okay." Oates's helper agreed with a sigh. "We'll dig up a security guard, send him to your cottage to get it."

"See that you do, huh?" Pepper said, only then turning on the smile for the official. "I have to have it aboard by T minus thirty at the latest."

"You'll have it, Commander."

The count stood at T minus one-hundred-nineteen minutes.

The Marine trumpeter climbed down from the bus. It was a relief to get off. He was still stiff, uncomfortable, more than a little ready to stretch his legs, flex muscles into arrangements impossible to achieve in a bus seat. It was good to get outside even though it was hotter on the macadam than in the blackest pit of hell.

"You guys got five minutes," announced a little Air

32

Force captain who looked like a blue bowling ball with a head. "Then you gotta' form up and climb onto that grandstand over there."

"Who's that little shit?" muttered the new flute player.

"Who knows? Who cares?" someone responded. "Air Force thinks it owns space."

The trumpeter looked eastward to get another glimpse at the bird. That's what he wanted to see. Today he didn't give a damn about the music, the long trip, even the promotion he had been promised. Right then he was interested only in the bird. There she was, shining gloriously in the sunlight with her giant gantry crane standing by.

It was a classic beauty-and-the-beast matchup. *Titan* was sleek and potent looking. *Titan* was awesome and, in a strange way, sexy. The gantry was ugly and functional.

"Think that big sucker'll ever get off the ground?" asked one of the drummers, a buck sergeant.

Percussionists were such assholes, reflected the trumpeter. Then he heard the mutter of distant thunder. He turned to see a dark, forbidding western sky.

Somehow it bothered him a lot to see that weather moving in. It wasn't the threat of another bus ride. It had nothing to do with the prospect of getting wet. It was the matter of getting the bird away. It seemed so important to him that *Titan* rise true today, that she fly safely and well.

"Get them tunics on!" came the word up and down the line. "Get them tunics and hats on. There's history bein' made here and it ain't gonna' be made up of a bunch of bandsmen in their skivvies!"

The trumpeter removed his red tunic from the garment bag, but before he put it on he glanced again over his shoulder at the menace rolling in from the west.

The man's face, replicated millions of times on television screens all over the nation—indeed, the world—was a familiar one. It spoke to the viewer in terms of honesty, candor, good will, and a level of expertise far beyond that of the layman on almost any subject one might care to name.

The voice was familiar, too, a trustworthy, friendly voice that nearly a hundred million Americans could recognize as readily as the voices of some members of their own family.

"Today, ladies and gentlemen," said Bill Waddell from *Titan* Television Central at Cape Canaveral, "we mark an historic departure in broadcast journalism, fulfilling a dream we've personally cherished for nearly a decade."

There was something wonderfully personal about Waddell's delivery. Long ago he had mastered a technique every broadcaster longs to add to his own bag of tricks—the ability to make his listeners, viewers, truly care about him.

"Dozens of times we've been given the privilege of bringing you up-to-the-second coverage of America's space liftoffs, watching a whole distinguished company of America's space heroes—Shepard, Cooper, Gill, Grissom, Glenn, Stafford, Young, the rest—as they were flung skyward, seeking the nation's destiny among the stars."

"Now back off," ordered Waddell's director in the control trailer. "Back off so we can get the bird over his shoulder!"

"Gotcha'!"

It was a terrific picture, dramatic, transmitted as if by magic into America's early morning breakfast room. Waddell's grizzled, still handsome features were perfectly highlighted foreground with *Titan* showing up gorgeously background. The sun still shone on her, glinting off her fair form.

"Today, ladies and gentlemen, you'll be hearing another voice, seeing another face, as the great fireball erupts to power *Titan*'s four and a half million pounds off the pad and into an orbit two hundred miles above this populous blue sphere on which we love and labor. Your correspondent will, today, briefly abandon the spectator role and will ride, as your representative, man's greatest achievement into the ante-chambers of the heavens."

"Cue four, now!" ordered the tech director in the trailer.

The image of *Titan* filled the whole screen.

"That old boy's a bit much, isn't he?" commented a network rep from Atlanta. "Ante-chamber of heaven?"

"How'd you feel if you were wearin' Bill Waddell's trousers this morning?" the producer retorted from his seat at the back of the control room.

"Don't rightly know," replied the younger man with a grin.

"Then show some sympathy, baby. Show sympathy for the man!"

The young security guard still felt rotten about what he'd pulled in the middle of the night. He wasn't one to enjoy being humiliated. Only a few hours had passed and he was emotionally bruised and bleeding from the rough going over he'd taken. It had come from everyone, not just his fellow security people.

"Shootin' up any space invaders lately?" they'd called out after him.

"What's the current bounty on senators?" someone else would join in.

"Were you planning to stuff him, boy, or was you gonna' get his head mounted on your wall?"

Well, to hell with all of them!

No matter what they said, he was making a contribution to the launch. He would have a role in the big show after all.

He pushed the jeep a little harder, made it go faster. His orders were specific. He was to get over to the cottage where Commander Pepper'd been staying. Security had already reached Pepper's wife, just arrived from Houston, on the phone. She'd meet him at the door with the log book. Then, he was to get the critically important book over to 39A as quick as he could move it.

Well, he wasn't about to screw up this time! One of the advantages of being security and knowing the Cape as well as he did was the fact that he didn't have to stick to the impacted, car-jammed roads.

"Go, you little sucker, go!" he shouted at the jeep. It wasn't a dune buggy but it was amazing what it could do in the hands of a man who considered himself an expert.

John E. Tillinghost and his wife Trina were in the first limousine. It was totally fair that he was chosen to go first. After all, wasn't he the principal creator-designer of the glorious craft? Others had been involved at various steps along the way but, generally speaking, *Titan* was the product of his fertile brain, the fruit of his intuition, the offspring of all those years of his study and research, the direct result of his stubbornness, or, as he preferred to call it, his inspired persistence.

"'Four-eyes' has won big!" Trina said to him as the Mercedes slowed down preparatory to their arrival at the gate near the largest viewing stand.

"What?" He had no idea what she was jabbering about.

"Don't you remember 'Four-eyes'?" she asked him, smiling broadly.

He started to shake his head. Then abruptly he remembered. It had come to him. He grinned over at her. "If only they were all here to see this," he said wishfully.

"Maybe they are," she pointed out to him. "Maybe they're all watching on TV."

They'd called him "Four-eyes" and worse, those miserable bastards, in years gone by, all through high school, but especially in the primary grades. John Tillinghost couldn't play ball worth a damn, spent all his time reading or playing with numbers, couldn't run fast enough to avoid their cruel jibes or, on many occasions, their fists and feet. It was a ghastly way to grow up and he'd hated it. "Four-eyes," or "Professor" they'd called him.

Trina was absolutely right. If they could see him today on TV, those mindless Neanderthals, they might feel envy themselves. "Four-eyes" was now fitted with contacts. He was well conditioned, trim, and well tailored. He would step out of the limo with his gorgeous, stylish wife into such stuff as dreams are made of. And right before their eyes he'd ride a lightning bolt of his own devising. In it he'd climb right up to the front porch of the stars.

"I'm tempted," he said, just as the car came to a halt before the crowded viewing stand.

"Tempted?"

"To thumb my nose at the cameras when I get out. I

37

could get all of them wherever they are with one nasty, abusive gesture."

Trina laughed in sympathy with what he called "his temptation." She knew, nonetheless, that John would never condescend to do any such thing. For old "Four-Eyes" would never take any such direct route to anything, any course of action that would expose him to criticism or ridicule, for those were the real phantoms her husband dreaded.

She smiled. She was happy. It was a triumph—John's day!

It was all limousines and choppers—a very high-class circus, indeed. The third whirlybird, a sporty French jet, was coming in with the insignia of the Saudi royal family splashed all over its side.

Chairman Locke's chopper with its Space Star logo was already on the ground and there were a couple of Air Force helicopters just coming into sight. Dallas oil man Jasper Tanner's private helicopter was off to the side, rotor blades still turning.

Closer to the grandstand, near the Marine Band, the sleek cars were gliding smoothly to the passenger gate and discharging their celebrities, some to board *Titan*, others to watch liftoff. It was a great show. The media people were having a field day.

Senator Leon Gill paced back and forth in the VIP trailer provided by the TV network. He was checking over his speech. He wore, for the first time in years, a NASA flight suit. He hadn't objected to the idea at all. As a matter of fact, he liked it. Despite the air-conditioning, he was sweating heavily.

It's one thing, he reflected, to speak to the Senate, the

38

whole Congress, to be out on the campaign trail scraping up votes. These days, even the TV camera, once a problem for a shy farm boy from Indiana, was no obstacle at all. It was simply that today he'd be speaking before people he considered his true peers.

Shepard, Glenn, Carpenter, Cooper, would be out there in the crowd. So would Cernan, Collins, Lovell, Conrad, and Young; so many of the old crowd. It would be no easy chore, making a formal speech to them.

The door opened. It was Ben Polikov.

Mame Gill was with him. Resplendent in the new pale blue dress, she just stood in the doorway and grinned at her husband.

"My God," she said, "but you do look terrific, Leon. Guess I'd forgotten just how sexy you look in that suit." Then, wrinkling her pretty nose in puzzlement, "It still fits?"

"They made me a new one," he admitted. "It was NASA's idea to make me a new one for today."

"You weren't supposed to tell," razzed Ben Polikov.

Mame herself looked terrific, fit, suntanned. Her snow white hair was cropped becomingly close. Her skin was firm. Her eyes were bright. She still had that terrific figure.

"Aren't you going to kiss me for luck?" she demanded, very much aware of her man's approving inspection.

"Hey, lady," he objected in fun. "You know I got a speech to polish up."

"Listen to the man. Isn't that a hell of an excuse? To forsake a girl at midnight in a strange bed, to go out running, nearly getting himself shot in the process, now he's too busy to—"

Gill interrupted the remainder of his wife's diatribe by stopping her lips with his own.

"Maybe I'd better leave you lovebirds alone?" asked Polikov in jest.

Abruptly, the trailer door opened and Ted Bassano boarded. There had been no knock, no called-in preparation, and there was no apology.

"We ready, Senator?"

"As ready as we'll ever be," Gill replied.

"Well, then, let's go. There's a space-happy world waiting out there to hear you."

Mame looked over at Polikov. "You know, Ben," she said. "He used to promise me that someday he'd sneak me along on one of these 'business trips' of his. I loved hearing him say it, but I honestly never thought the day would come!"

"Come on, lady!" said the Senator, smiling happily at her.

Thus they went out to meet the crowd, TV, the nation, and the heady challenge of the skies.

With the aid of the steward, a strikingly handsome man with thick, wavy red hair, they were belted into their space couches in the first-class cabin. Princess Constance and Prince Conrad found themselves the fifth and sixth individuals aboard on their level.

First seated had been a gray-haired man with a stunning young wife. He was pointed out to them as Doctor John Tillinghost, designer of many, if not most, of the systems that comprised the space shuttle.

Next had boarded a prince of Saudi Arabia, an elegant man wearing the *kaffiyeh* and *'igal* of his culture. He was accompanied by his son, a good-looking youth of about twelve, dressed in the same exotic fashion.

"See," Prince Conrad said to his wife after they'd been strapped in place and the steward was occupied with the

40

next pair, America's former Ambassador to Great Britain and his wife. "I told you we shouldn't have rented the wagon."

"What?"

"We're banished to the third row." He gestured eloquently to the Arabs who were seated above them, closer to what would become the front of the passenger compartment.

Princess Constance wanted to laugh but it didn't come. Instead, she squeezed his hand. And for a moment she felt, along with her love for him, very, very frightened. It was neither a pleasant nor a familiar sensation. It was as though cold fingers had suddenly taken hold of her heart.

She tried to think about Willi the Bold, as she jokingly called one of her ancestors, a bellicose figure who seemed to have known no fear whatever.

Wherever or whatever you are now, Prince Willi, she said within herself, I could use a little of that aggressive stupidity of yours, that genetic perversion that made you brave!

There are certain turns a jeep, no matter how skillfully driven, will not make on sand, on an irregular, off-road surface.

The young security guard rushing back toward Pad 39A innocently attempted such a turn and, as his vehicle flopped over like a discarded toy, he was flung beneath it. The flight book flew clear.

For a moment the jeep lay there atop the helpless youth, wheels spinning.

"Christ Almighty!" someone shouted from the line of vehicles parked just off Kennedy Parkway, "he's pinned under there!"

"Call it in on the CB," shouted someone already running toward the mishap. "I think this poor bastard's had it!"

The count stood at T minus forty-one.

It was a short speech. It had been planned that way. Upon its completion, even before the applause subsided, Senator Gill and his wife would be rushed at top speed to join their fellow first-class passengers already secured in place in the passenger module. Only then would Gill's shadows, his Secret Service watchdogs, leave him temporarily as vulnerable as other men.

It was, as the press asserted later, not one of Gill's better addresses. He said all the usual things—the obligatory clichés, the tired nostrums favored by those who seek to pay their dues to the rest of society by political service. Further, his concluding remarks were almost predictable, knowing who he was, what he'd done, and what he sincerely believed.

"I am convinced," Leon Gill's strong clear voice rang out, reverberating to the farthest corner of the world via media, out across the flat scrub earth of the bleak island on which Kennedy Space Center was erected, "this bird is as safe as the flight of any commercial airliner in the United States today. Once again our nation has taken the lead in introducing a new concept of travel to those who would care to use it. The steamboat, the train, the automobile, the airplane, and now the spaceship have all begun their inaugural voyages from our beloved American soil. I am proud to play a role in that prideful progession!"

"Sorry this took so long, sir," apologized the technician, handing the log book to Pepper.

"Somebody play catch with it?" the pilot commented, noting that the cover was scuffed, several pages dog-eared.

"The guard had an accident getting it over here."

Pepper said nothing for a moment as he flipped through the book, making sure it was complete.

"Security guard flipped his jeep," the man added.

"How is he?" asked copilot Sager.

"Not good, we hear."

"That's a damned shame."

Pepper seemed satisfied with the condition of the log book.

"Wish the poor guy well," he said.

"Will do, Commander."

"And tell him thanks."

"Right, sir."

Sager had wondered if Pepper would get around to saying thanks. He was glad he'd done so.

There was a great deal of waiting built into the whole process. While the fuel was topped off and while a whole succession of important checks were made—a few manual, most automatic—all parties were alone with themselves.

Astronaut Judy Langenberg tried to keep her passengers loose, in good spirits, although from time to time she caught herself getting distracted, just a little bit worried about Karen. In one sense, at least, Judy wished *Titan* were going up another day.

Leon Gill and Mame settled in happily. Leon reminded his wife of a teenaged boy as he excitedly re-explained for at least the tenth time everything around them in the shuttle.

At Launch Control, Tim Oates, a man of considerable

competence and authority, watched it all happen with an unaccustomed feeling of impotence. Events seemed to be rolling forward with an accelerating rhythm and power of their own. Oates felt strangely disconnected, detached from it all. It was, for a few moments at least, a weird, unfamiliar ritual conducted in a peculiar, meaningless gibberish.

In the passenger module, tourist-level, Carl and Mary Fittipaldi from Springfield, Delaware County, Pennsylvania, winners of a "Space Getaway" promotion, found the excitement building to an almost unendurable pitch. Carl, an auto service manager, had raced stock cars, skydived, scuba-dived, and, whenever the opportunity arose, engaged in anything daring—anything physical and exciting. He was on top of the mountain!

The doctor, in surgical greens, shouldered his way through the trauma room door. His big face registered fatigue. His eyes looked blank.

"Well?" demanded Bob Murchison, Kennedy Security Chief who'd rushed over to be with his man.

The physician shook his head angrily. "Forget it," he muttered.

"What?"

"Lost him, damn it! I'm sorry."

Murchison said nothing.

The doctor continued angrily. "What the hell can you do? A human skull isn't made to handle that kind of pressure. There are some things . . . you . . . you just can't ask the human body to do!"

Titan had, although few would see it that way, already claimed a life.

It was just inside T minus six minutes. Everything was

44

on automatic. They had moved without incident through the built-in holds, and the radio exchanges between cockpit and Kennedy Launch Control had subsided to an occasional terse inquiry.

The 139,000 gallons of liquid oxygen and the 370,000 gallons of liquid hydrogen had been topped off. The gantry crane had been wheeled back and the gimbals had been uncaged, leaving only a few shearable bolts securing the shuttle to its mounts.

Then, abruptly, Pete Sager's voice came crackling over the radio, breaking the tense, expectant silence.

"Kennedy, it's good to know those tricky little computers of yours are jabbering to each other."

Was he thinking of the shuttle Columbia's first launch back in '81 or was he alluding to the persistent rumors that had earlier that morning flown around the Cape?

"What's that you say, *Titan?*"

"Glad to know that Houston's little computers are busy talkin' love talk to each other and that we're gonna' get out of here on time."

"We copy."

At the Johnson Space Center in Houston, eavesdropping from two-thirds of the way across the continent, Jim Taggart, Cap-Com for the *Titan* flight, laughed out loud.

"What's the matter?" asked a distracted, scowling Flight Director Lou Chandler, who'd been deep in a minor technical problem.

"Old Pete's really pumped up. You know he can't keep his mouth still when he's excited."

"What's he saying now?"

The big man looked as though he were ready to duck.

"Said our computers are talking love talk."

"They better be!"

45

"Leave it to Pete to put it in those terms."

"Just see that he doesn't say anything X-rated on national TV after he's ours," warned the Flight Director.

In minutes, just as soon as *Titan* left the pad, the Kennedy Space Center at Cape Canaveral would relinquish control of, and communication with, the spacecraft. Houston Control, with Cap-Com Jim Taggart, an astronaut himself, would take over. Chandler would be Flight Director for the duration of the short flight.

Taggart chuckled again.

He knew that for all the noisy grumbling about Sager's runaway mouth and his unorthodox ways, for all the jibes about "Pistol Pete," that Sager was one of the best of the pilot-astronauts, the jet-jockeys. And of that group, there was no one Scientist-Astronaut Taggart was going to miss more.

"Speakin' of pumped-up or pumped-down people," drawled Chandler, still standing by Taggart's console, "I hear you been makin' less than enthusiastic noises—in a way, ominous noises—around here."

"What's that?"

Taggart looked up with surprise written all over his lean, dark features.

"I realize this isn't an optimum time to discuss it, but before you commit yourself to a certain course of action I've heard you're considering, I'd appreciate it if we could talk. I really favor us havin' a little heart-to-heart—real soon."

Taggart was startled. Who had told old "Stone Face"? Who'd informed the Flight Director he was thinking seriously of leaving NASA? Was it Bess? Could it have been Everett? Might it have been one of his group, the so-called "Excess Eleven"?

For a moment Taggart said nothing. Then, finally, he

46

responded. "Okay, boss man. We'll talk. But not now, huh?"

"Not now," Chandler agreed, shambling back to his own station.

The image of the shuttle on the huge screens flanking the even larger map spread across the front wall of Mission Control at Houston was repeated in homes all over America.

The circus atmosphere back at the Cape had subsided. Those who had come to garner publicity had already wrung all the visibility possible out of the situation. The show had been taken over by the bird and by the clock. The Marine Band was no longer playing. The traffic on the base and for miles around had stopped moving, and the official "Hold in Place" order was in effect.

Although it had been done an even hundred times before with almost the same vehicle and dozens of times with other, less sophisticated spacecraft, the excitement was enough to stop the breath in the throat, to freeze the heart in the rib cage.

On previous occasions, the only puny humans riding on the head of the inferno were tough, determined professionals, an elite corps of those who had looked at Death, measured it calmly, and then said, "It's a possibility that can be minimized with planning and training and systems. Therefore, we'll face it!" The men, and lately, women, who'd steered the lightning bolt had always been a breed apart, designated with that special, almost magical, name—*astronaut!*

This trip was unique and the nation—the world—knew it. Along with *Titan's* crew would ride ordinary citizens of the Planet Earth, people made of mere flesh and blood. Though wealthy, well-known, distinguished,

47

well-connected, or just plain lucky, they were cut from the same bolt as those who sat riveted in front of their TV sets to watch and empathize.

The digital displays moved inexorably forward.

Two minutes forty-one seconds!

Two minutes forty seconds!

Two minutes thirty-nine seconds!

The Marine trumpeter sat leaning forward in his seat on the grandstand, the muscles in his legs already toned for him to jump to his feet at the appropriate time. His red bandsman's tunic was so damp from perspiration that it felt as though it were cast concrete.

In front of the press grandstand, an utterly drained PR man, who'd gone through the whole emotional gamut from A to Z and back again, gnawed a pencil and, for the first time in almost thirty-six hours, was uncharacteristically silent.

One minute three seconds!

One minute two seconds!

One minute one second!

One minute!

Fifty-nine seconds!

Would the clock keep moving? Or would there be some last minute complication that would send the whole technological houses of cards tumbling—something that would send the breathless nation back into a limbo of waiting?

Thunderclouds still rolled, threatening, over the mainland to the west of them.

Twenty-eight seconds!

Twenty-seven seconds!

Twenty-six seconds!

Peter Sager looked over at his pilot-commander. Pepper was, even at that very instant, looking across at him. Both men winked almost simultaneously. Then, both chuckled.

Seven!

Six!

Five!

Four!

The bolts were snapping and shearing off beneath the gigantic rocket engines. The unendurable fires were building within the great *Titan*'s belly.

Three!

Two!

One!

"We have liftoff!"

3

A GIGANTIC blossom of the most vivid flame bloomed and grew inside an immense enveloping structure of billowing smoke. The center of the fireball glowed with indescribable brightness. Parts of the huge launch pad—railings, alarm boxes, telephone mountings, stanchions—began to glow redhot and even melt.

As if out of sync with the flash of fiery ignition came the great, rolling torrent of sound, seeming full seconds delayed, an earsplitting roar that out-thundered a thousand Fourth of Julys.

Grass and small brush for at least two thousand yards in every direction burst into flame, smouldering, charring, all but disappearing altogether in the blast of 6000° Fahrenheit.

Titan hurtled bravely skyward!

"Looking great, *Titan!*" crackled the enthusiastic voice of Launch Director Karl Heinz, eager to express his boundless enthusiasm before Houston Control stole his bird from him. "You look fantastic!"

"Much obliged for the lift, Kennedy!" acknowledged Command Pilot Pepper, in effect bidding the Cape official farewell.

"Glad to be of service. This is Kennedy out."

Ever accelerating, *Titan*, with her trio of rocket hand-maidens, punched a neat hole in a puffy cloud and then reappeared streaking skyward on the other side, triple-exhaust plumes and fringes of fire marking her triumphant path.

Passenger Leon Gill, observing the fiery ascent on the closed-circuit TV monitor mounted on the forward, now upper, bulkhead of the first-class cabin, was loving every instant of it. It was as if he were peering directly over the pilot's shoulders. Gill squeezed his wife's hand as the craft in which they rode seemed to leap from earth's gravity like a living thing.

Mame squeezed back.

How lucky can one man get? Gill asked himself as he was fired like a circus daredevil higher and higher into the heavens, leaving the nasty weather they'd earlier worried about, many miles below. They were already traveling far faster than the speed of sound.

Life was good, rich, a source of vast delight. And now he'd been granted an opportunity to revisit one of its highpoints, its greatest joys, with the woman he loved.

Neither of them spoke. It would have made little sense at that point. They were simply too choked with feeling to get the words out. The shared squeeze of the hand said all that needed to be said.

The nation and the world watched *Titan* scale the morning sky. She seemed to grow smaller and smaller as she rose, thundering ever higher. But there was no diminution in the process. She was a giant—a wonder!

She was toasted with morning coffee, cheered with rusty morning voices, and wished Godspeed with a whole galaxy of prayers.

51

"Look at that beauty go!" shouted the President of the United States where he watched with a handful of staff members in the Oval Office.

The television cameras were still locked on her.

"Put me through to the cockpit right now!" he ordered impatiently, reaching for the phone on his desk. He was an impulsive man, strong, hearty, quick on the trigger.

"They'll connect you shortly, Mister President," cautioned an aide. "Houston claims they have to get the craft established in orbit before they'll put any call through."

"It'll be a few minutes, Mister President," put in an ex-astronaut on the White House staff, "before the pilots have a—"

"Remind 'em I'm the damn President," the man behind the desk interrupted testily. "And *this* President doesn't like being kept waiting!"

Looks were exchanged.

"Yessir, Mister President," one of them said and got busy again on the telephone.

"Workin' manual on that?" Pete Sager called over to Pepper, noting that Pepper was flipping switches.

Pepper nodded his head affirmatively, too absorbed in what he was doing to talk.

Sager wasn't altogether sure it was a good idea to execute anything manually at this particular point in the mission. Somehow, keeping the whole business on computer, on automatic, at this early stage seemed a better idea to him. There was something so exhilarating about the early moments of a launch that one's judgment, timing, could easily be warped by feeling, by the inescapable emotional high. Even the best could manage to screw up under such circumstances.

*   *   *

The old man sat staring intently at the television screen. Only his jaw moved slightly to indicate he was alive, awake. He wasn't a particularly old man, but there was something ravaged looking in his face and there was a kind of blankness, suggesting a home from which the family has already started moving out.

The only sound in the sunny parlor was the voice-over commentary of the television broadcaster. The image of the beautiful space vehicle had become barely more than a flickering dot on the screen as *Titan* burned downrange.

"They got off fine, Mister Langenberg," said a tall black woman in nurse's white, who stood behind her patient. "They're right up there."

The man said nothing. There was no sign that he'd heard. He simply kept staring, even as the broadcast returned to the format of anchorman chatting with guest experts and commentators.

The nurse moved around in front to see that her charge was all right, that the light blanket was neatly tucked in around his knees, wondering if it might not be time to trundle him back to his room, now that *Titan*, carrying his daughter, was airborne. Suddenly she was startled.

For on his sunken cheek—the cheek of one who'd been a powerful, strong-minded man before Alzheimer's Disease had made a mockery of his strong physique and his once confident, incisive manner—a single salt tear ran, impelled by gravity, drawn forth by . . . by . . . who could tell?

"It's all right, Mr. Langenberg," the nurse assured him softly. "It's all right. They're up there in fine shape. Not to worry!"

*　　*　　*

It was T plus one-minute-fifty-one seconds when it all began.

A flashing red light labeled *Engine 3* began its intermittent warning. It claimed that Main Number Three was failing to produce full thrust.

"What the hell!" shouted Jay Pepper. "Check that!"

Sager quickly consulted the backup indicator, one of the spacecraft's network of redundant systems.

"Got it there?" the commander demanded.

"Negative," answered the copilot. There was no indication of malfunction on the cockpit backup indicator. "Want me to check Houston?"

Pepper shook his head.

Pepper's pulse rate had increased sharply. He'd been a solid 90 just seconds earlier. Suddenly he was 135. Sager held steady at 95.

"You're looking gorgeous, *Titan*!" called Cap-Com Jim Taggart. "This is Houston Control and you're looking fat and sassy from where we sit!"

The pilots on *Titan*'s flight deck exchanged glances. That confirmed it for the moment. They must have been getting a faulty indication. The number three engine had to be okay!

Most of Judy Langenberg's charges looked like the entertainers at Madame Tussaud's Wax Museum. A full two-thirds of them looked frightened, awed, all but frozen stiff as the great rocket charged heavenward.

Judy knew the drill by heart.

Her charges were then experiencing, like her, two G's of acceleration. They were passing Mach 4.5, or four and one half times the speed of sound. Shortly they'd clock seven times the speed of sound.

She smiled reassuringly at several of her passengers who were looking at her right then. She took the microphone of the cabin intercom.

"Right now you should be feeling as though there's a full-grown adult sitting on your lap. But please," she went on, with a grin, "don't let it go to your head!"

There was a ripple of relaxing laughter.

That's what you're here for, lady, she told herself. That's why they let you tag along!

Houston broke in at T plus two-minutes-thirty-one seconds.

"*Titan*, advise RTLS abort. Initiate at T plus 256 seconds."

There was an instant of stunned silence at this advice to Return-To-Launch-Site.

"Say again, Houston!"

"Advise RTLS abort, initiate at T plus 256 seconds."

"Roger. Copy," responded Pepper numbly. "Recommend RTLS abort at T plus 256."

"*Titan*, you've got Main Number Three down in power." Jim Taggart was working to keep his voice calm, matter-of-fact, as though he were passing along a clear weather report on a takeoff. "You're reduced a good bit from full thrust. Say about thirty percent."

"Jesus Christ!" said Pepper, shaking his head.

"Could use *Him*," Sager agreed.

It took several seconds to really let the notion sink in.

They had ninety seconds to act or not to act. Both men on the flight deck of the spacecraft were all too well aware that many things could go wrong with RTLS. What was involved was a difficult pitch maneuver four hundred miles downrange at four hundred thousand feet

55

at a speed of Mach Five plus, with external tank still attached and the remaining shuttle engines still firing.

It was a bitch!

They'd have to pitch around, regain control of the shuttle aerodynamically, and head back for Kennedy. There was no room for error—not a millimeter!

John Tillinghost, in the first-class compartment, was counting to himself. He'd felt the peculiar bucking and jerking and began to sweat. He could all but feel the individual beads of perspiration as they squeezed from his pores.

As he gazed at the big screen above him, there was something about the way the shoulders of the two pilots hunched there in the foreground that told him all was not well. Just from the way they leaned, he sensed problems.

Would they abort?

His mind rejected such an idea. He was imagining things. Despite the fact that he'd designed most of the components, the general configuration of the craft, he'd never been in love with flight. Perhaps his imagination was a mite too vivid. Perhaps he was too familiar with the possible consequences of a single tiny malfunction, the catastrophic implications of a single instance of metal fatigue.

Could the pilots handle an abort procedure in the unlikely event that they should be called on to execute one? He'd never been confident of the technique. It had never actually been tried. Getting rid of the main tank while pitching back for the launch site was rough. Ten months back they'd nearly lost a crew and a shuttle just testing the preliminary stages of such a maneuver. And that hadn't been a bird carrying fifty-two other human beings. During the separation of the fuel tank phase, the pilot would have to keep *Titan's* nose pointing down, and this would be done manually to keep from pitching too far. Too much pitch and . . . and . . .

John Tillinghost didn't want to finish the formulation. He'd seen enough fire for one day. He had to face it. There was no real reason for alarm. The spacecraft was ascending just as the textbook directed. He could easily have been imagining what he thought was going on up forward. The unsettling truth was that he was plain, old-fashioned scared and here, on the craft he'd designed, there was clearly no place to run.

"Anything wrong?" Trina asked, noting the strained expression on his face.

He shook his head emphatically. He couldn't summon the spit to speak.

Houston came on again with the carefully controlled voice of Jim Taggart.

"*Titan,* we verify thirty percent loss of power in Main Number Three, apparently due to a ruptured fuel line or fitting. Request to initiate RTLS. Set clock countdown to first pitch maneuver at T minus fifty-five seconds. Mark!"

Pepper obediently reset the cockpit clock.

"Roger. Copy."

Then forcefully he asked the question that had been very much on his mind.

"Is AOA an option?" he demanded.

Sager was nodding his head *yes,* vigorously, hopefully.

There was dead silence as the clock moved ever forward. Pepper had asked if the power in the spacecraft's engines was adequate for them to do a single orbit and land (Abort-Once-Around) at the Northrup Strip at the

White Sands Missile Range in New Mexico. The AOA would, in his judgment, be far safer because they wouldn't have to turn the shuttle around with the external fuel tank still attached.

"Answer, damn it!" he muttered between clenched teeth.

The clock advanced relentlessly. He had a whole forty-nine seconds!

Something was wrong!

Judy Langenberg's nose had picked up the scent of burning rubber. It was a strong odor—unmistakable. Her passengers way back, far below her as the shuttle was angled, seemed restless. She could see them squirming in their seats as if trying to get away from the odor that was beginning to leak into their pressurization system.

Judy reported immediately to the cockpit on the intercom.

"Getting fumes back here," she said quietly. "Burning rubber."

"We copy," came Sager's chalky voice.

"I'll do what I can."

"Be sure you monitor for toxic effects."

"Affirmative," she said. "Doing everything I can," she reported.

"Know you are, babe," Sager said calmly. "Know damn well you are."

"I'm truly sorry," said the Assistant to the Mission Director. He was utterly sincere and his voice reflected that sincerity. "The flight crew is totally engaged in flying their mission at the moment. We'll ring through to *Titan* just as soon as they're free."

58

"This is priority," explained the caller. "I don't think you understand."

"We understand very well, sir."

"It's the President of the United States," came a very impatient, second male voice from the other end of the connection. It was an uncomfortably familiar voice.

"And I'm very sorry," the NASA man replied, working hard to maintain politeness and to keep his cool. He could see his boss and others outside his glass enclosure, get some idea of their agitation and concern. "It's physically impossible at this point in the flight to fly the spacecraft and to chat with—"

"The President's on the line."

The Assistant to the Flight Director lost it at that moment. Something suicidal, something desperate took over.

"It can be . . . it can be the Pope for all I can do about it!" he snapped. "Or the Queen of England! When we get things under control, we'll call *you!*"

He broke the connection, marveling even as he did so. He'd just hung up on the President of the United States. My God, he gasped to himself, what a way to start a day!

Chandler knew he had a hairy choice at best.

But it was an obligatory procedure. They'd been through it time and time again with the engineers. They'd laid out every possible malfunction with every variety of detail they could come up with. They'd spelled out all the choices, weighed all the odds as carefully as they were able. Then, they'd fed the whole ponderous mess into a battery of the most powerful computers they could come up with.

RTLS seemed the advisable maneuver. Executed cleanly, crisply, professionally, it would probably work.

And Jay Pepper and Pete Sager were the best possible men to carry it out.

"Again?" asked Taggart.

"*Order* them!" Chandler growled. "Bludgeon them if you have to. *They gotta' do it!*"

RTLS! RTLS! RTLS! RTLS! RTLS! Chandler kept repeating over and over inside his head.

Even as he repeated it over and over like an aspiration, some mumbled invocation to the gods that look out for spacemen, Chandler was wondering whether the technicians, the engineers, had considered that fifty-foot-long tank in there. Had it been factored in? If RTLS occurred, those poor suckers in the tank would have the damnedest ride of their lives!

Carl Fittipaldi had never been so exultant in his whole life.

Sure it stunk in the tourist cabin. Sure it felt as if some fat guy were sitting on him. Sure there were sensations coursing through him the likes of which he'd never felt before. But that was part of it all, wasn't it? That was part of living.

Here he was, ticket all paid for him and for Mary. Here he was enjoying it with some of the fattest cats in the land in exchange for a ticket in a lottery.

Well, baby, he said to himself. If you die right now, at this very second, you've still been to the top of the mountain!

Then he spoke to the spacecraft itself. Go on, you big beautiful bastard! he urged the incredible machine around him, pushing it with his will to climb, leap, drive, soar into the endless heavens opening above them. Go like a big-assed bird, he urged *Titan*. Go!

"What's going on up there?" demanded a puzzled,

angry, hurt President, finally replacing the telephone receiver back in its cradle. "They all crazy aboard that flying brickyard?"

"What's wrong, sir?" asked one of the braver presidential aides.

"I *am* the President, aren't I?"

Bill Dye, Special Space Adviser to the White House Staff, had a sick sensation in the pit of his stomach.

He had no hard information to go on. As far as The Voice of *Titan* (the name given to the PR program at Space Star for this mission) and the TV commentators were concerned, things appeared to be in excellent shape. But there was something about not taking the President's call that made him sure that *Titan* was having problems. It was a hunch but it was a strong one.

"They're in a critical portion of their flight, Mister President," he pointed out, trying to get rid of the look of affront in the President's eyes. "Maybe they're . . . they're having trouble."

Had the angry Chief Executive really been listening, he might have heard the gravity in the speaker's tone of voice. He might have known from his space adviser's face that whatever had transpired between cockpit and Oval Office could have been the result of true stress, not indifference or deliberate discourtesy.

However, the President was listening only to his feelings. "If you think they got trouble up there," the big man behind the Oval Office desk said nastily, "just wait'll they get back down here!"

"*If* they get down," Dye responded with tears welling in his eyes. "*If* those poor bastards get down!"

He didn't understand it. There was no evidence except for his instinct and the crew's unwillingness to accept the presidential call. Yet the certainty of trouble was building in his mind—in his guts.

Abruptly, William P. Dye, Space Adviser to the President, wheeled and walked purposefully from the room.

"Bill, you get back in here!" called the President.

Dye kept on walking.

"Dye!" came the President's gravelly voice again, louder, tougher. "Get your ass back in here!"

But the executive order, for all the vigor of its delivery, went unheeded.

Sager approved the way his skipper was handling things. There was no sign of panic, indecision, wavering of any sort. Pepper was working in absolutely straight, true lines. He was showing more than his fair share of "the stuff."

Sager agreed with Pepper, too.

RTLS was not the way to go. With a little luck they could make AOA and bring it in. Textbook procedures weren't everything. Sometimes "the cook book," or astronaut's manual, could be wrong. That's why they'd put men in the cockpits of spacecraft. And, flashing red lights or not, Pete Sager was still happy to be one of those men!

Houston was back on the line.

"This is Houston Control. We command you to initiate RTLS. T minus sixteen seconds and counting."

"Is AOA possible?" Pepper shouted. "We indicate affirmative!"

"RTLS minus nine, eight, seven . . ." continued the voice of Jim Taggart.

"Fuck it!" snapped Jay Pepper, turning off the radio. He nearly took the switch off with it.

"We actually got ten seconds to exercise RTLS option," indicated Sager like an automaton. Truly he wanted to give Pepper every option, every opportunity.

Commands from Houston could still be heard as the backup unit flipped on. The words hadn't changed, but they sounded angry, cold, resentful.

"We command you to commence RTLS immediately. Do you copy, *Titan?*"

Pepper shook his head vigorously and bit down on his lower lip.

"*Titan,* do you copy?" Taggart kept repeating.

"This is no yo-yo on a string, Houston," said Pepper. His face showed agitation, anguish, almost, as he wrung the words out. "This here's a spacecraft and there's a commander on this flight deck. Do *you* copy?"

There was a brief silence.

"We copy!" acknowledged Jim Taggart.

Pride!

That was the operative word.

David Locke was feeling pride. He was about to bust the buttons off his shirt. Space Star was the biggest, most incredible thing on earth. To hell with Frank Borman and his airline. To hell with all those other people who'd given him a hard time. He had *Titan*.

He leaned back luxuriously in his first-class seat and savored his triumph, G's or no G's!

David Locke, for all of the forty-nine years that sometimes obsessed him, that drove him to frenzies of trying to prove things—in the office, on the racquetball court, on the track, in the bedroom—was a winner.

Pride. That was clearly the word!

Sager, not a conventional believer, uttered, nonethe-

63

less, a prayer of thanks. For a spacecraft computer display showed that an orbit would be possible if the number three engine, still putting out some thrust, continued to function at the same power level.

"We got it, Jay," he said to Pepper.

The commander nodded grimly.

Of course, if there were any further atrophy of function, any diminishment of thrust, the shuttle would have to be ditched somewhere else in the world, maybe an ocean, a jungle, or, if their luck took a turn for the better, a not-long-enough runway next to a hard, flat, desert somewhere in Africa, Asia, or Australia.

"I don't know what the hell we're gonna' do with it," said Pepper, "now that we got it!"

Titan, stricken but how seriously yet to be determined, was in orbit.

4

TITAN was spinning around the earth in low orbit. That was a given fact!

The meeting in Houston was an improvised one—hurry-up, yet well attended. All the section heads either relinquished their seats to be present or sent subs to meet Chandler. The principal contractors were represented. There were technicians, engineers, medical people, backup astronauts, and a group from Space Star. Oates and several other top Space Star reps were still on the plane, or back at the Cape. Tillinghost and Locke, of course, were aboard the spacecraft.

Lou Chandler, looking like a rough-cut, old-fashioned school teacher, stood with a sheaf of reports in his hand, a serious, deeply worried look on his face.

The room became silent for him.

"Well, gentlemen," he began. "We have quite a pile to wade through!"

"Somebody oughta' fry Jay Pepper's ass but good," put in one of the Air Force liaison people from the back of the crowded room.

"*He's* flying the damn shuttle," said someone else, rushing to the *Titan* skipper's defense. It wasn't hard to guess that the defender, like both *Titan* pilots, was Navy issue. "Could you do any better?"

"At least I would—"

"All right, can it!" ordered Chandler, breaking in. "We got work to do. I don't want to hear anybody raggin' on anyone else around here or I'm gonna' do a little myself. And as some of you'll be glad to tell, my raggin'll make yours seem like nothin' at all!"

If there was one thing about Lou Chandler, it was that, elemental and rough-hewn as he was, he knew how to keep a meeting on track, how to make people work together. He was a supervisor who exacted a maximum amount of work in a minimum interval of time or heads started rolling. Everyone knew it and everyone responded accordingly.

"The question on the floor right now is, how do we get our spacecraft down with a full, safely livin' complement of passengers?"

"We're on target with the AOA approach," volunteered a Rockwell representative. "Let's start with that."

"AOA's the answer," put in someone else.

"What the hell else is there?" asked the chief of the medical team. "Whether we want it or not."

Chandler nodded his head in agreement. "Fair enough," he said. "AOA is obviously what we've been given, like it or not. The obvious rarely gets anybody pullin' hair too hard. But between us and a successful AOA lies a hell of a lot of homework and damned little time to do it in. We've got to work out and prove the track on this new orbit. We've got to work closely with the flight crew to see what can be done about the pollution that's gettin' into the tourist-class compartment. Is it life-threatenin' or not? And if it proves to be, what can we do about it? Where can we move 'em?"

"Do we have any idea of how it's getting in, Lou?"

"No way we can know," interjected another of the contractor's people, "'til we get flight crew in there to eyeball the situation."

"We got flight crew in that compartment already," Chandler pointed out. "We got Astronaut Langenberg. She's fully qualified on that system."

People exchanged looks on that one. Chandler was not the one any of them might have predicted as spokesman for any female astronaut. All through the development of the shuttle program, no one had pushed the women harder, made things tougher for them, than Lou Chandler. It had never shown up as outright opposition. Lou was too politically astute for that. It had simply been a case of working them harder, demanding more of them, than would have been expected from any male in the program. Some were strident about it, claiming loudly that Chandler was the grandaddy of all male chauvinists. Others, pro-Chandler, were convinced he rode the women hard because he felt that was the key to their gaining full acceptance. All agreed that Lou and Judy did not constitute a mutual admiration society.

"There are other problems," he pointed out. "With the engine burnout and the bumpy ride into orbit, we're going to have to check the spacecraft over thoroughly to be sure she's suffered no serious damage."

"What do you have in mind, Lou?"

"The obvious place to start is heat protection. Did the uneven firing of the number three engine cause any tile damage? Did the leaking fuel in any way compromise adhesion of the tiles?"

"What else?"

"Then there's the question of the airframe. Any dam-

67

age there? There was a hell of a lot of vibration—more than we ever anticipated."

"I don't think we got much to—"

"And I don't want guesses," Chandler broke in. "We don't get paid for guesses."

There was a long silence.

"I want our psychology boys, our medical team, to go over both the voice tapes and the medical telemetry to see if they can detect any human factors we have to brace for. We're facing," Chandler noted, very tight-jawed about it, "a sort of flight deck revolution. You will remember, gentlemen, that our boy Pepper, with the apparent agreement of his second-in-command, told good old Houston Control to take the traditional flying screw in the legendary rolling donut!"

Someone snickered.

"What's the time on this, Lou?"

"We got one orbit," said Chandler tersely. "The answer is, we do it immediately or just a little bit sooner!" He studied the men surrounding him. As he saw them, they were some of the outstanding technical talent in the world.

"Now let's hop to it!"

They did what he told them.

"I really bit the bullet," commented Pepper. There was a note of wonderment in his voice.

"What?"

"Blowing up at them—refusing RTLS."

"You did right," said Sager. "And you weren't alone in making the decision. I back you."

"They'll hang my ass out to dry."

Sager seemed to take his time in responding.

"It's always nice to have an ass left to hang," he said. "We wouldn't have made RTLS."

"Think we'll make AOA?"

"Not sure at the moment," Sager responded honestly. "Don't think we know enough about our condition."

"What about Tillinghost? Think he'd have anything to offer? He built this thing."

"Not a bad idea," Pepper acknowledged.

Sager wasted no time. He got Fisher, crew supervisor of the first-class compartment, on the intercom. "Need one of your passengers on the horn."

"Now?"

"Absolutely. But don't worry. He's in seat number one. Should be able to reach him with your own head-set."

"Tillinghost?"

"That's right. Like a little technical advice."

It was difficult to read Ron Fisher's silence. But somewhere in it there must have been an unspoken question.

"Going to get him for me?" insisted the spacecraft commander.

"Going to get him, sir," Fisher came back, feeling very much part of a military operation, something he was not at all used to.

There was a pause—a long one.

"This is John Tillinghost," came a voice.

In the most technical of terms, Sager got on the line and gave the designer a summary of the situation. He read off all the relevant readings from cockpit instrumentation and gave Tillinghost a quick rundown of their present status. He also briefly summarized the interchange between *Titan* and Houston.

"What about the tiles?" Tillinghost asked. He was

69

being very careful about what he said. He didn't want his wife or any of the other passengers to know what he'd first guessed and just had confirmed.

"As you know, sir," Sager came back. "We've got no easy way of determining that."

"Your . . . levels seem all right," the man on the other end of the connection observed, reviewing things.

"Fuel?" asked Sager, recognizing that Tillinghost was trying to be discreet in what he let his fellow passengers overhear.

"That's right."

"Fuel levels are . . . almost nominal."

"What's your advice?" Jay Pepper broke in. "We'd like your assessment of the situation, sir."

Tillinghost spoke softly. He betrayed no apparent nervousness or lack of confidence. His words, however, were sobering.

"Not sure, gentlemen, that we're . . . sound enough structurally or environmentally to do AOA. Before we consider that, we should eyeball the brickyard."

"We copy," Sager acknowledged, trying to indicate to the man in the first-class passenger compartment that he fully understood him.

The two pilots looked at each other.

"How's the tourist section?" asked the skipper.

"I'll check it out," Sager said.

He shifted the selector to station four, Astronaut–Payload Specialist Langenberg.

"What's your status back there?"

"Odor's still building," she replied, speaking softly. "I have a number of people nauseated. If I had more space and zero G's I'd like to move 'em out so I can see what's venting back there."

"Not a prayer for several more minutes."

"We'll work on it, Judy," said Sager. "Call you back shortly." Deliberately he clicked off the selector switch.

"What the hell was that?" challenged Pepper.

"Let's not discourage the lady," Sager said.

For an instant Sager got the notion that Pepper was going to flay him alive with the "I'm in command" speech. But Jay Pepper said nothing. He simply kept working with the ailing spacecraft.

In the tourist compartment the odor was clearly getting worse. There was a burning of the eyes and irritation of the mucous tissue. Several of Astronaut Langenberg's charges toward the rear of the compartment had become nauseous even before the advent of weightlessness.

Some were calling out to her.

She clicked on her microphone and spoke to them all. "Ladies and gentlemen, what we're experiencing now is the residual odor of the engine burn." She was lying.

"How do you know?" someone asked.

"I've been out here before," she said.

Another voice called encouragement, consent.

At that moment she loved her charges. They were friendly, fair-minded people out for a good time. She was determined to do the very best she could for them.

"In a few moments," she went on, trying to anticipate a little, "I'll move a few of you from the back of the compartment where the smell is worse."

"How are you going to do that?" someone asked.

"Where are the seats?" came another challenge.

"In a few minutes we'll be weightless and you all won't have to stay in your seats."

There were no further challenges. Judy held the live microphone in her hand for a few additional seconds.

71

She couldn't see them all with the compartment in that particular configuration. But she could hear some of her charges gagging and retching.

How strange, she thought to herself. *How strange, what we human beings will undergo for a few seconds of thrill, to be brother to birds!*

Then she corrected herself. *What self-respecting bird would be out here in such a fix?*

Billy Couchera, chubby, sleek, and balding, was, despite his lazy-eyed, almost indolent appearance, a sharp, perceptive newsman. He was one of the best. Sitting there in the press gallery at the Houston Space Center, doodling naked female boobs on one of the yellow legal pads he constantly carried, he became aware of something.

Abruptly, he sat up, energized, on the alert.

It was tough to put one's finger on, but something had clearly changed in the scene he was there to watch. Something was different about the pace, the overall intensity of what was going on in Mission Control. He sensed it as though a bell had gone off inside his skull.

His own expression tightened. He shifted his weight, put his two feet firmly on the floor. He sat leaning forward, watching intensely through the plate glass. It was impossible to overhear anything. They had the audio turned off.

First of all, he reflected, there was altogether too much movement in the big room. There were supervisors moving from console to console, looking very grim, very focused.

There was none of the joking, rather laidback camaraderie that often seemed the dominant mode during

72

such missions. There was little smiling. Everyone was leaning into the situation.

Couchera craned his thick neck trying to catch a glimpse of Chandler. It hadn't taken him long to learn how to read Flight Director Chandler's face. Despite Chandler's hard-boiled qualities, despite the fact that he was by far the most competent man at the Space Center, the nice thing about Chandler was that he was easy to read.

All he could see was the back of Chandler's big head. He was in his regular position, but there was something unusual about him—something fueling the alarm bell ringing in the watching newsman's mind.

It was the way Chandler's neck had retracted, tightened. It was as though something inside the wise old ex-astronaut had told him, "Batten down the hatches! Get ready for a fight!"

Billy Couchera was crawling the walls. Something was going on in Mission Control. And he'd be damned if he wasn't going to get the story!

Aboard *Titan*, there were striking contrasts.

While those on the flight deck sweated, struggled with the crisis, while those in tourist retched and gagged, hoping vainly for clean air, the fortunate few in first-class, except for John Tillinghost who knew better, luxuriated in blissful ignorance of their danger.

"This is so incredible," murmured Mame Gill, eyes shining with excitement.

Grinning characteristically, her husband responded, "Didn't I tell you it would be?"

"For years."

"Glad you came?"

"Is it like your flight?"

He chuckled. "My ship was a little more cramped than this one," he admitted.

Somehow the Gills looked and acted like a pair of newlyweds off on a lark.

In the next row forward, then actually above the Gills, relaxed David and Essie Locke. The Lockes had become millionaires almost overnight when forty-nine-year-old David, dabbler in investments in and around the aerospace industry, had finally struck it rich with the somewhat unexpected popularity of passenger shuttle flights. As President of Space Star Enterprises, Locke had acquired from NASA four space shuttles, each with a fully booked schedule of monthly flights over a period of three years. Although the criteria for SSE's passenger selection procedure were a matter of controversy, there was little question that Locke, through crafty and persistent entrepreneurial skills and excellent timing, singlehandedly bailed out NASA from near extinction by turning up a gigantic new market for NASA's spacecraft.

"What are those thumps?" Essie demanded.

"What thumps?"

"It's vibrating strangely."

"Stop playing neurotic."

Essie was a neurotic. David Locke was utterly convinced of it.

"It's strange," she persisted.

"What the hell do you know?" he hissed.

The atmosphere in the compartment was calm—comfortable. The Luxembourg Royal Couple held hands, smiling. Another royal personage, the prince of the House of Saud, spoke quietly to his young son, explaining just what was happening. The youth listened intently

74

even though he may very well have known more about the shuttle than his parent.

Others sat oblivious to anything ominous, chatting quietly, enjoying each other's company. There could be no awareness of a tiny, undetected fatiguing of metal, the sudden, catastrophic deterioration of a metal valve fitting that had, in effect, hung them out over the abyss.

Carelessness had not caused it. Weather conditions had no responsibility for it. There had been a miniscule flaw in the metal, an unplanned for, impossible to anticipate failure at precisely the wrong moment.

At T plus nine minutes, fourteen seconds, the oxygen masks dropped in the tourist class section of *Titan*.

This more than anything prompted panic to spread in that compartment.

"Ladies and gentlemen," Judy Langenberg called out over the public address system. "We have a temporary low-level contamination of the cabin air supply. Thus we're offering oxygen if you find it helpful. If you've forgotten the procedure I demonstrated to you before liftoff, may I repeat it for you now?"

Without warning, one of the passengers left his seat.

"Please remain in your seats, buckled in securely," Judy called out to him.

The man was a catcher for the New York Yankees. There was a glazed look in his eyes, one of desperation.

"We're undergoing a state of maximum G loading."

Like some tree-dwelling creature, some misplaced higher ape, the man who had reclined in seat 13, on the port side, was climbing upward toward the forward end of the compartment, a vertical climb, using other seats to give himself a purchase. The effort was tremendous.

Judy could see the way his eyes bulged, could see the distended tendons in his thick neck.

"Please, sir."

He paid her no heed, but concentrated on fighting the tremendous pull of gravity.

On the flight deck there was still a major problem to be faced, a grave decision to be made.

Houston was insistent on Abort-Once-Around, a single revolution of the earth, a returning to a predetermined backup site in New Mexico. The pilots of *Titan* weren't anywhere near as positive.

"Can we make it to *Spacelab* and get down again?" asked Pepper of his second-in-command.

Punching a preset computer program, Sager got a green light there in front of him.

"Affirmative," he said. "That is, assuming we can keep this level of thrust."

Pepper nodded his head. "Then we've got to risk it," he said grimly.

"Agreed."

"At least *Spacelab* can do a visual inspection to see if we can survive reentry."

"What about taking some of our people off?" asked Sager.

Pepper's eyes widened with surprise.

"Couldn't we offload some?" Sager continued. "They're catching hell from the fumes. May get worse. If we're forced to it, we could move some into the cocktail lounge and offload the rest on *Spacelab* . . ." He didn't have to finish. He could see that Pepper had caught his idea, was turning it over, evaluating it.

"Not bad," said the skipper. "The trick is to sell it to Houston and to *Spacelab*."

Without hesitation Pepper pushed the pilot-to-ground button.

"Houston, we have evidence of physical damage to *Titan* near engine number three. There are fumes in the tourist passenger section. We have fuel to rendezvous with *Spacelab* to check out *Titan* or for rescue if things get really dicey. You copy?"

There were several seconds of silence. Somehow the silence seemed heavy, disapproving.

"Hold on for a moment," came Taggart's voice.

The pilots looked across at each other. Both were visualizing some kind of debate at Houston.

Taggart's voice came to them loud and clear.

"We command that you immediately initiate an Abort-Once-Around, apogee one hundred five miles. We have a ground crew waiting for you at White Sands."

Before there could be a response from the flight deck, Judy Langenberg cut in. "It's getting worse here. Most aren't using oxygen. I have a crazy climbing loose in the compartment. Can we evacuate into first-class once we get zero G's?"

That did it. Action had to be taken on the spacecraft. It couldn't be handled from the ground.

At precisely T plus fifteen minutes, twelve seconds, without further exchange with Houston, Spaceship Commander Jay Pepper cut off the space shuttle main engines, jettisoned the external tank, and they were headed on a trajectory that would take them to *Spacelab VII*. The passengers felt a forward surge in their seats and were suddenly weightless.

"The pilot of that shuttle is in open rebellion," claimed Henderson, backup flight director. He was totally amazed. "I never would have thought it of Jay Pepper."

77

"Claims Tillinghost agrees with him," Taggart put in.

"Tillinghost's on holiday," Henderson came back.

"His knowledge isn't," commented Chandler.

"You agree with him?" asked Kohler, one of Space Star's liaison personnel at Houston.

Chandler shrugged. "It's *his* responsibility," he said. "And the cream's been spilt, hasn't it?"

Aboard *Titan* there was a thoroughly festive air in the first-class compartment. The Prince of Saudi Arabia amused his son and the Gills by placing his closed drink container and straw in the air in front of him, leaving it suspended. Others were delighting themselves by gently wafting their weightless arms in the air.

John Tillinghost was, however, in a cold sweat. He could interpret too well what had happened. He understood with too great a degree of clarity all that could go wrong and what the penalty might be for any one of a thousand possible errors.

Within twenty seconds of becoming weightless, the designer of *Titan* reached for a white bag and vomited.

"This is Captain Pepper," came a voice in both passenger compartments. "I'm speaking to you from the flight deck of *Titan*." It was a reassuring voice, deep, sure of itself, without any sign of agitation or excitement. "We wish to welcome you aboard the space shuttle."

"Some welcome," called one of the passengers from what was now discernible as the rear of the tourist compartment. "Nice stink."

"We experienced a textbook launch," the captain's voice told them. "During the ascent, however, we had a bit of a problem with engine number three which is adjacent to the tourist passenger cabin. Nothing serious.

As a precautionary measure, we will temporarily move the tourist passengers to the first-class cabin so we can take a closer look. We have a go for an orbit and should have things straightened out within a short while. Sorry for the inconvenience."

The intercom clicked off.

On the flight deck, Jay Pepper took a long, deep breath. "Was that . . . okay?" he asked Sager.

It surprised Sager that he asked. Usually Jay Pepper wasn't the sort to ask the opinions of anyone else.

"First rate. I didn't hear any nerves leaking out from under. You had it altogether in hand."

"Glad of that."

To some extent, the commander's speech calmed things down. Moments before, the tourist cabin, despite Judy Langenberg's best efforts, had been a scene of great confusion. The fumes had continued to thicken. The rear part of the compartment seemed to be enveloped in a yellowish haze. Most of the passengers were floating free, bumping around into seats, into each other. There was the excited babble of voices.

"Is this *it?*"

"You think he's telling the truth?"

"How do we get to the other compartment?"

"*Please*, everyone," Judy called out. "*Please*. I've got to have your attention."

"Listen to the lady!" shouted Fittipaldi, the service manager from Pennsylvania.

"Listen, damn you!" shouted Fred Waite, the Australian adventurer. "Our lives may depend on it!"

The sudden intervention of Judy's two allies seemed to do it. Things quieted down to a reasonable extent. Judy took advantage of the slight break.

"I want you in your seats, using the oxygen."

Reluctantly, people began trying to move back into their places.

"Those of you in the extreme rear," she said, "will come out first."

With the assistance of Fittipaldi, Judy opened the hatch to the airlock, a small compartment designed for docking with *Spacelab*. A closed hatch at the forward end of the airlock led currently to the cockpit. A closed hatch just above the one to the tourist section led to first-class.

"I'm sending them up, Ron," Judy announced over the intercommunication system.

"Come ahead," came Fisher's voice over her headset.

Judy Langenberg led her tourist passengers one by one in the awkwardness of zero gravity. Many of them were nearly as well known as the first-class passengers: Claude Meakin, Speaker of the House; Missy Grace, movie starlet; Kurt Sommers and daughter, two of America's outstanding screen actors; Jack Yost, top-seeded tennis star. One by one they floated into the airlock.

With about one-third of the passengers evacuated, a surge of panic welled up in the compartment when the airlock hatch slammed. Judy fumbled for the microphone to announce that the airlock was full of people and that they were closing it to minimize leakage of fumes into the upper compartment.

But before she could manage to quiet things, with dozens of weightless bodies bumping around the entryway to the airlock, one of her passengers lost grip on a handle and found himself slammed hard against a seatbelt holder that impaled his left arm.

"Oh, my God!" he shouted.

Globules of blood spurted from the arm and deflected off wall and seatbacks, dispersing the weightless blood into thousands of tinier red particles that seemed to fill the contaminated air.

The victim was Marshall Sutphen, pitcher for the New York Yankees, battery mate of the man who'd earlier gotten out of control, scaling the cabin before weightlessness had made such a thing theoretically possible. Ben Polikov, nearby, pulled off his shirt and applied a tourniquet. Polikov was quickly saturated with blood himself, speckled thoroughly. Other passengers bruised themselves as they sought to avoid the spreading droplets.

"We've got to have order here," Judy insisted.

"Come on, you people," shouted Fittipaldi, who had stayed back to help, sending his wife Mary in the first group moving to first-class. "Settle down!"

Combined with the shock of seeing a fellow passenger injured, the commands of Astronaut Langenberg and the supporting orders of the brawny Fittipaldi seemed to bring the shaken people back under control.

"Can you handle him?" asked Judy of Polikov, who had taken the injured man into a set of vacant seats and was better securing the tourniquet on his arm.

"I'm no doctor, but I think I can control this bleeding," he responded grimly, not even looking away from what he was doing. "You got your hands full, lady. I'm okay."

"My pitchin' arm," moaned the ashen-faced Sutphen as though he'd lost the arm altogether. "That's my . . . my breadwinner."

"Take it easy, pal," responded Polikov, trying to calm the man. "It's gonna' be okay. I promise you."

Struck by the big man's gentleness, his air of quiet competence, Judy turned her attention back to her temporarily calmed passengers. For a moment they were stabilized emotionally, although the physical atmosphere in the cabin was getting markedly worse.

"Can we do it without EVA?" Pepper asked his copilot. "We have to know how those tiles are around Main Three back there."

"Don't know," Sager admitted. "But where we gonna' get the time? We can't get out there on a single AOA."

"That's for sure," Pepper came back, shaking his head. "That's the hairiest part of the dog for sure. If we're AOA we have to take it on faith."

The two pilots were discussing the problem of examining the tiles on the outside skin of the shuttle. Each of the 30,761 ceramic tiles bonded to the spacecraft played a critical role in the shuttle's high temperature reentry of earth's atmosphere. As a matter of fact, it was felt that the loss of just a few tiles on some portions of the craft's surface during a temperature peak up to 2700° Fahrenheit could lead to the loss of the vehicle and its whole complement.

EVA, or Extra-Vehicular-Activity, seemed to be the best way to go. What both men were thinking at that particular moment would involve suiting up Sager and sending him out through the airlock to carefully examine the exterior, looking for missing tiles. If it was necessary, he could effect appropriate repairs out there in zero gravity.

"If we go that route," Sager said thoughtfully, "we have to stay in orbit long enough to effect the repairs."

Pepper shook his head to indicate understanding. The

smiling confident skipper of the press conference seemed to have disappeared altogether.

"What are the options?" he asked.

There was a brief hesitation. Then, suddenly, Sager's eyes lit up.

"Ian Stafford," he said.

"What?"

"Ian can eyeball us from *Spacelab!*"

Pepper, still biting his lip, relaxed noticeably, almost smiled.

"Think you got something," he said. "Think you hit the jackpot although we still got to sell it to Houston. My ass is already in a sling!"

"More than one ass in a sling," Sager pointed out. "More than one."

Couchera's round, normally bland face was beet red. He had to keep wiping his glasses. It was warm in the small press room. He wondered if it was his own very excited person steaming up the atmosphere.

"Look," he began, leaning across the narrow table, "you guys are always bullshittin' about how open our space program is compared to the Russians. Ever since there was space to write about, I heard all this crap about how if our moonman's suit had blown up, we wouldn't have covered our asses."

"You heard right," said one of the NASA PR types.

"What about now?" the reporter demanded, giving the hotshot facing him no place to go. "What about now? What about we put our money where our mouth is?"

Couchera was ill-suited for making eloquent statements of any kind, but he was wound up—on the trail of something. He would have his say.

The two men facing him looked very calm, very grave. The bastards didn't even seem to be sweating in their crisp white shirts.

"We have nothing to report," one of them said quietly. It almost sounded credible.

"That's bullshit!" Couchera responded quickly. "You guys should be honest with the people who pay for this—the public. I can tell something's happening in there. There's a rhythm in that room, a quality of movement I can read. I can tell by Chandler biting everybody's head off, the way he's running in there. He's already changed one shirt and he's sweating through the second."

"Look, buddy," said the second NASA man. "When we got news, I assure you, you'll get it."

Couchera shook his bullet head.

"I'm going to break it," he announced, amazing himself even as he summoned the words, strung them together. "I'm going to break the story that something's wrong with *Titan*."

Both men, under considerably less control than they had been moments before, tried to answer at once.

The first said, "You can't do that!"

The second began with, "You're going to look like a stupid fool!"

"I don't give a shit," Couchera came back. "I'm willing to bet my damn career on it!"

"You'll bet it on reading a pantomime through a thick piece of plate glass?"

"That's right, pal. That's right."

The two PR types exchanged glances.

There was a long pause.

"Can we strike a deal?" asked the first man in a quiet, unemotional voice.

Couchera took his first full breath in what seemed a very long time. It tasted sweet.

"Maybe," he said. "Just maybe."

The first coughing, gasping consignment from tourist had been placed in the intimate little cocktail lounge at the aft end of the compartment, a posh environment equipped with luxuriant velvet pillows, some anchored down, a few floating free. The room had ports all around. Although these windows were yet dark, with the whole passenger pod still resting in what had originally been designed as *Titan's* cargo bay, the room was opulent, comfortable.

There were a few cracks from those traveling first-class.

"Did all these folks pay for their seats?" Jack Garson called out when the first group of displaced passengers floated by. He was smiling as he put the question, but his eyes glittered nastily and there was a harsh edge to his voice.

"Having a little trouble below, Mister Garson," said Ron Fisher, the steward. Fisher was a smooth article, very much in control of situations.

"We're all glad to help," said Princess Constance.

"We second that," came the familiar voice of Senator Leon Gill.

It was difficult to find places for all of them. Even the second group of ten were a bit difficult to accommodate.

It was the arrival of the third and final group, however—nine in all—that precipitated a real problem in the luxurious, previously untouched luxury compartment.

Ben Polikov, assisted by Wilfred Noel, a general in the U.S. Army, guided the injured Marshall Sutphen through the crowded compartment when suddenly the bloodied shirt, rigged as a tourniquet, was somehow dislodged.

"Oh my God!" screamed Essie Locke. "He's bleeding!"

The man was indeed bleeding at zero gravity and globs of blood floated free, rendering the whole situation even worse than it was.

Additionally, the compartment had taken on a definite odor. Despite the use of the airlocks, the best efforts of Langenberg and Fisher to prevent contaminating the first-class atmosphere, some of the noxious, yellowish smoke seemed to have entered with the refugees, clinging to clothes, hair, flesh.

"This is horrendous! I object to the whole thing!" Once again it was Garson.

"I agree," stated Ambassador Leslie Burton, just named to the Court of St. James, to become American Ambassador to the United Kingdom.

"What'd you want us to do, choke to death?" demanded Missy Grace. "That what you wanted?"

"Might have been a good idea," put in Garson's wife.

"Come on, people!" Steward Fisher broke in, using the cabin intercom turned up as far as he could boost the gain. "We've got work to do. We're all in this together. You hear me? We're all in this together!"

If only temporarily, Fisher's sobering message seemed to take hold, to mute them for a few seconds.

There was little question, however, that what he said was true. He was speaking the truth. They were together aboard *Titan*, an ailing *Titan*, and they were a long, long way from home.

It was hard to believe.

The commander of *Spacelab VII*, the first ESA space vehicle configuration to be cut loose from its orbital transporter to whirl in its own orbit around earth, listened to radio traffic between *Titan* and Houston. His long face, serious to begin with, reflected even greater gravity as the conversation crackled back and forth between the ailing spacecraft and the ground.

Having been trained as an astronaut by NASA, Ian Stafford had no trouble visualizing everything that had happened to that point. What concerned him most of all was the fact that he knew—all too well—the members of *Titan's* crew.

"You look worried," commeted Henri Lubac, one of *Spacelab's* crew members.

"I *am* worried," Stafford responded almost absently. He sat hunched forward, listening intently for more transmissions.

Lubac had free-floated into the compartment.

"You . . . you believe it's really . . . bad?"

Stafford smiled quickly, bleakly.

"Let's say . . . there's ample reason for concern."

The French member of *Spacelab's* crew, unlike his British commander, had acquired his training for *Spacelab's* mission in the Soviet Union as one of the growing number of non-Russian cosmonauts. Thus his technical familiarity with American space hardware was more limited than Stafford's.

"You think . . . she's all right?" asked Lubac finally, after a pause. He was reluctant to raise the issue but wanted to assure himself his commander was not worried to excess.

"I hope so."

The Frenchman jockeyed himself around so he could see Stafford's face. He could see it upside down clearly

87

enough. Nearly two months in space had given him a reasonably good facility at reading human features from all sorts of peculiar angles.

"You still have . . . have . . . like you say, a . . . torch burning for her?"

For the first time in the brief conversation, Stafford glanced up. His gray eyes looked straight at where the other spaceman floated. They were compelling eyes, part of a strong personality.

"Henri, she's the mother of my child. That's the beginning and the end of my personal concern in the matter."

"*Pardon*, Ian."

"My professional concern," continued Stafford, "that I hope I can translate into action, is the possibility, as part of the complement of another space vehicle, of rendering aid."

"How?"

Stafford shook his head.

"I'm not sure."

Basically, *Spacelab* had become little more than a satellite, a series of tin cans parked in orbit. Loaded with scientific equipment, a whole variety of experiments, testing procedures wih commercial applications, *Spacelab* was not able to achieve orbit or return to earth by herself but had to wait patiently for the space shuttle *Atlantis* to come up and carry her back to earth.

Yet, if there were some way. The tall, solemn Englishman sat wondering, racking his brain to work out a way in which he and his associates could do something—anything—to aid the stricken craft.

For a few seconds his mind created for him a picture of Judy, tough, dark-eyed, determined little Judy.

He was startled by the intensity of the emotion he felt in response to the image.

"Damn!" he muttered.

"*Pardon?*"

"Nothing," Stafford growled, continuing his radio watch. "Nothing at all."

There were portable life support systems aboard but they were all in the shuttlecraft itself. Judy decided there wasn't time.

Oxygen masks floated all over the compartment, each connected by an umbilicus of rubber tubing to the spacecraft's backup oxygen system. They were still operating.

As she made her way aft, she could move from mask to mask, backing up her own breath control so as not to get too much of the fumes that now filled the area and made it almost as difficult to see clearly as to breathe.

"You got another light?" asked passenger Fittipaldi who insisted on remaining with her as a backup. "Buddy system," he'd described it.

"We don't need one," she said. "You just stay back here with a mask on."

"What am I, a spectator?"

"You aren't trained," she pointed out firmly.

Fittipaldi said nothing. Little did the lady know that Carl Fittipaldi, auto service manager on weekdays, was a trained scuba diver, rock climber, hang glider pilot. Beneath his sports shirt and doubleknit slacks, Fittipaldi had as fit and trim a forty-eight-year-old body as one could find outside the space program, the armed forces, or Stillman's gym.

"You're the boss," he responded.

The objective at this point was to get aft, to make some

kind of evaluation for the pilots as to whether the rent or leak—whatever it was—could be closed to seal off the odor, the fumes, from what might have been a ruptured fuel line in the passenger module life support system—a problem seemingly unrelated to the engine three burn-out.

Cautiously, the young astronaut began making her way. She propelled herself slowly along the aisle, trying not to make contact with anything that might injure her or deflect her in another direction. She held a powerful lamp set on indirect so as not to deflect brilliant light back into her eyes off the millions of tiny, yellowish droplets that seemed to fill the air—yellowish and, in some instances, reddish brown from the injured man's blood.

"Don't forget to breathe, hotshot!" Fittipaldi called out to her.

Judy didn't answer. She kept herself focused on the job at hand.

She did, however, take his advice. Eight times, in the short length of the fifty-foot compartment, she paused, sought and found an emergency oxygen mask, and inhaled the invigorating gas.

Any nervousness she may have felt, any of the dread she had felt when her passengers almost broke on her, was dissipated. Now she was dealing with a technical problem, a rupture or leak, the sort of thing she was trained for.

"You okay?" Fittipaldi called out.

He was a decent person—a genuine help.

"First class," she responded.

She was almost back to the apparent area of problem. The light was not doing the job especially well. It was simply too bright for the chemical fog that had formed. There was too much reflection off the droplets.

"What's the matter?"

"Tough to see."

"Want me?"

"Sexist."

He laughed.

Having directed the light as low as she could manage, Judy turned her body over in its weightless state and began to pull her head and shoulders down toward the cabin baseboard. She could hear a faint hiss.

It was a tight squeeze to reach what seemed the source of the problem. The light was more hindrance than help. She let it go. Her fingers groped for any sign of a breach in the bulkhead. She had wondered if it were anything caustic or toxic in any way. Yet she'd left off gloves, allowing her fingers to feel things, to get some accurate reading of the trouble. She had wriggled, by this time, deep under one of the seats, trying to make a gulp of oxygen last as long as she could.

Time to get another breath, her body told her. She'd pushed it a little.

But she could not move. Somehow she was wedged in.

No longer holding the lamp, she tried with both hands to extricate herself from the narrow quarters between the outboard seat and the bulkhead.

It was futile. She was jammed in solidly.

The anguish of not breathing became the dominant sensation. It was torture. Pushed to the limit of her endurance, she was forced to give in. She inhaled. Almost immediately she began gagging and choking.

"Hey," she heard Fittipaldi call. "What's a'matter? Hey!"

Then she felt strangely light-headed and things began going around as if she were riding the centrifuge again. Then everything went dark . . .

"Hey! Hey!"

5

COMMANDER Pepper's voice came clearly from the speakers. He spoke calmly but forcefully.

"Houston, we've talked over the problem here with John Tillinghost and with President Locke. We have decided that it's negative on the AOA procedure."

"Say again?"

"I repeat. It's *negative* for AOA until we get a good look at our heat protection capability."

There was a pause while the second flat refusal was given a chance to sink in. Then Pepper's voice continued.

"Houston, request authorization to go through with the planned rendezvous with *Spacelab*. We request that *Spacelab*'s crew survey us visually for tile damage. Further, we request information on the availability of shuttlecraft to effect rescue. Over."

It was a bombshell!

There was what seemed a lengthy lapse in communication.

Then, for the first time in the mission, the rough, raspy voice of Lou Chandler was heard over the radio circuitry.

"*Titan*, this here is Houston Mission Control, Flight Director Chandler speaking. I'd like to know just what the hell's going on up there. You people are still under orders to fly your mission under the direction of this space facility and with the guidance of its personnel. Over."

Lou Chandler was a man who neither pulled punches nor walked around obstacles to avoid confrontation.

"Houston," Commander Pepper came back calmly, reasonably. "I believe you know very well what's going on. We have a damaged spacecraft. How badly it's damaged is anyone's guess right now. We have an injured passenger. We just had to pull one of our crew members out of danger. On this flight deck we've got two qualified flying officers who join the spacecraft's principal designer in believing that completing AOA maneuver without visual inspection and possible repairs could have a catastrophic result. Therefore, Houston, charged with the personal responsibility for the mission and the lives of those aboard, we are continuing to frame the mission up here and would appreciate your final support. Over."

It had been a hell of a speech. And it seemed to take Lou Chandler several seconds to prepare an adequate response.

"We copy, *Titan*," he said at last. "We copy and we emphatically disagree. After full completion here, we strongly advise you to follow through Abort-Once-Around and get your bird back on the ground. Our engineering officer assures us you should be all right *if* you follow instructions. Over."

"We won't land, Lou, without visual inspection of affected areas," answered Pepper. "Other decisions will have to depend on the total information package."

"In addition," the softer, less nasal voice of copilot

94

Sager came on, "we cannot attempt a landing with any personnel in the lower passenger compartment. The atmosphere there is not breathable."

"We copy, *Titan*," said Jim Taggart, responding to Chandler's hand signal that he take over again.

Looking over at Lou Chandler's face, Jim Taggart had the strong feeling that, for all the gold in Fort Knox, for all the luscious young womanhood in Hollywood, he wouldn't willingly sit in the Mission Director's chair. It was like seeing a whitened, sun-bleached skull behind the apparently healthy features of a living person. There was a weary, immensely discouraged look for a moment on the man's face—a look totally uncharacteristic of the self-confident, utterly unflappable Lou Chandler they'd all come to know and trust.

"We copy and we continue to disagree," said Taggart, trying to back up his boss as best he knew how.

"We certainly do disagree, Jay," Chandler added almost sadly.

It was clear that Chandler was not trying to bluster or threaten. He understood what his flight crew was feeling. For a long time he'd been fully aware of the feelings of many of NASA's flight personnel—feelings that Houston was intruding altogether too frequently into the business of flying the shuttles.

Yet there had to be control—a modicum of discipline. Wasn't that so?

The disapproval seemed to hang there between earth and sky for an interval that approached twenty seconds.

"Where do we go from here, Houston?"

"Clarify please, *Titan*," said Taggart.

"Where do we go for a reviewing authority?"

It was a fascinating question, but by no means an easy one to answer. The chief executive officer and the high-

95

est ranking technical officer of Space Star Enterprises were both aboard the shuttle, in apparent agreement with the pilots. Chairman of the Senate Committee on Space and Aeronautics was also aboard. The NASA administrator, in a rather ambiguous position as far as *Titan* was concerned, was out of the country, in China.

There was really only one answer—difficult as it would prove to be, tough as Houston would find it to swallow. Taggart could tell by the look on Chandler's face, he knew what that answer would have to be. The mission, what was left of it, utilizing all the assistance Houston could marshal for it, had to be guided, flown, from the flight deck of *Titan*. The hairy decisions would have to be made by the flight crew, backed up by their cabinload of experts and authorities.

"What do you want to do, Lou?" asked one of the major controllers, off-mike.

"Let's have it, Lou?" demanded Pepper.

Taggart looked expectantly at Chandler.

For a few seconds, Chandler seemed immobilized in his seat. Then, without warning, he became sharply alive once more and he spoke with the gruffness of a grizzly.

"Let's find out how soon we can get another shuttle up there. Jay and Pete are waiting for the information."

The tension slacked off a little. It had become clear that *Titan* would call its own shots.

There was something brewing all right. There could be little doubt about that. Jack Summers had been in the Commissary, putting down some of the preliminary groundwork with Katie, the new girl in Continuity. He'd been happily bullshitting her with the old routine about how badly his wife misunderstood him, when MacFadden came in to fetch him.

"Doesn't a man get a damn minute to himself around this network?" he demanded on the way back to the studio.

MacFadden, typically, had little to say except one shocking statement.

"*Titan*'s in trouble."

"What?"

Titan in trouble? That was like saying Bill Waddell was in trouble. That meant that *their* man, the network's number one man, current dean of American newscasters was . . . was . . . in jeopardy somewhere . . . somewhere out there whirling around the world he'd so expertly covered night after night.

"What the hell's going on?" demanded an ashen-faced Jack Summers as soon as he got inside the studio.

"Houston just released the word: *Titan*'s got problems," said Mae, the number two editor. "Problems described as, and I quote, 'Potentially mission threatening.'"

"Mission threatening? They're only up for two orbits."

"That's what they said."

"Damn!"

"That sounds to me," the woman continued, her voice trembling slightly, "like NASA gobblygook for life threatening."

"God!"

Normally, Television News Central handled catastrophe as if it were yesterday's leftover soup. Tragedy they took in stride—assassination, war, famine, all the rest. A snide remark here; a touch of gallows humor there.

This time it was different. Bill Waddell, the man who

normally filled the center seat at the big anchor desk, was out there in the sky. That fact had a way of bringing the shuttle and anything that might threaten it right onto the set.

The copy was in the teleprompters, the cameras and control room were manned, and Jack Summers, powdered down, tie straightened, slipped into a seat he had lusted for, but which at that particular moment felt damned uncomfortable.

The floor manager threw him a visual cue, the camera light winked on.

"I'm Jack Summers sitting in for Bill Waddell. NASA and Space Star have just announced that *Titan*, America's inaugural passenger space vehicle, is experiencing 'mission threatening' difficulties. As of this moment we have not learned what these difficulties may be, but here at Television News Central we are deeply concerned about our own veteran colleague, Bill Waddell, riding the thunderbolt!"

Locke found it difficult to speak. He'd been briefly consulted by the flight deck over the phone. But what was happening now? What was going on? The fumes, the crowding, the horror of all that blood from the injured ballplayer. There was a growing sense of panic within him.

"Something's got to be done!" he managed to get out, facing Ron Fisher.

"Something *is* being done, Mister Locke," the steward answered him. "A great deal, as a matter of fact."

"Then why the hell haven't I heard about it?"

Fisher smiled. The steward was good at keeping his feelings under control, making his face do tricks on cue.

"It's pretty busy up there. Surely you, even more than

98

the rest of these people, can appreciate that. These men are professionals. They need to work without too much interruption."

"Take it easy, Locke," interrupted Leon Gill from across the aisle. "I have great confidence in those boys up front."

"I want to know what's being done!" There was an edge of panic, not terribly well hidden, just under Locke's voice. His wife Essie was saying nothing. She simply sat in her seat, fist pressed into her half-open mouth.

"The pilot will inform us at the appropriate time," said Fisher. "And I'm sure his explanation will satisfy us all."

"Whatever he decides will be the way we go," Gill volunteered.

That seemed to do it.

Locke all but pounced on the Senator.

"Who are *you* to talk that way to me?" he demanded. "Ex-astronauts are a dime a dozen. Don't you realize, Gill, who I am! I'm Space Star. I'm the whole show. I'm Space Star, lock, stock, and barrel. I can own you, buy or sell you without batting an eyelash!"

David Locke, in the throes of inner turmoil, a panic he had no idea how to deal with, lashed out at Leon Gill, feeling somehow that if he could sufficiently flail the old space hero, his own fear, his own terrible discomfiture, would somehow be mitigated.

Gill simply laughed. "It doesn't do much good up here, Locke, all that anger—big talk. We're both passengers and Jay Pepper is commander. You can yell and threaten all you like, but there's not much likelihood of buying or selling anything up here. Like good little girls and boys we have to wait and see what's going to develop."

99

Locke looked around as though seeking support.

Tillinghost was out of the compartment, something that had initially unnerved and angered him. The Prince of Luxembourg was leaning back with eyes closed, looking very relaxed and comfortable. The other prince, the Arab, was clicking his worry beads and holding his young princeling's hand. Only the yachtsman Sprigg of the first-class passengers nearby seemed disposed to take his side or even to look vaguely sympathetic, but Locke couldn't stomach the man.

"You . . . you tell your . . . damn pilot . . . I want to know what's going on—now! That's me, David Locke, his employer. I don't want any gibberish about 'doing all we can' or 'we'll inform you at the appropriate time.' I want information, solid, hard information right here and now. Do you hear me?"

"Please sit down, Mister Locke."

"And you can also tell him I will not put up with the inconvenience of having all these other lesser people from tourist cluttering up this first-class compartment. I want it clear that—"

"Damn it! I've heard enough!" interrupted Leon Gill. Suddenly, the veteran member of the Senate was transformed into a very angry Marine Colonel, icy-eyed, strong-jawed, totally in command of himself and the situation. "Locke, I want you to sit on that couch and keep your mouth shut! I want you to zipper your—"

"You can't talk to me like—"

"Shut up, mister! Just because you're falling apart, turning yellow, I'll not have you bothering my wife and the rest of these good people. And if, mister, you don't stop this disgraceful behavior, I'm going to personally install you in the padded cell back there they call the cocktail lounge!"

100

With that, Gill, more than slightly irritated, nudged the man—gave him just the least suggestion of a push.

The effect was startling.

Locke, a fair-sized man, went spinning backward across the compartment, heels over head, to bounce off the far bulkhead.

It was not an especially violent action, seeming to happen rather slowly, like some ballet move filmed in slow motion. On the other hand, there was something so outrageous and flamboyant about a man going through such a movement as the result of a tiny push that it had a sobering effect on everyone.

They were in a different environment—an unfamiliar element. There could have been no clearer, more dramatic explanation of the fact that aboard *Titan* a new set of rules, a totally new set of norms, prevailed.

Recovering what was left of his poise, Locke made his way back to his couch and rebuckled his seat restraints.

Ron Fisher, with an unobtrusive gesture, made his gratitude known and mouthed the words, "Thank you, sir."

Gill nodded his head in acknowledgment.

"You're still feisty!" Mame Gill said softly to her husband.

"Someone had to be."

"Are you . . . nervous?" she asked him.

He considered for a moment. "Apprehensive," he admitted. "I'm apprehensive."

"I'll have to remember that," she said devilishly. "That's a good way to duck, isn't it? *Apprehensive*." She smiled. It was not a happy smile. It was a resigned smile—apprehensive.

The word was out at Patrick Air Force Base.

101

Everywhere one looked, airmen, civilian personnel, transient Marines were gathered in sober little clumps around television sets, radios. Nobody had much to say. The tone was somber.

The Marine trumpeter, just about to board a plane for Andrews, asked someone.

"What the hell's going on?"

The airman shook his head. "Nobody knows. But it seems like *Titan*'s in danger."

The Marine inhaled sharply between his teeth.

"There's a TV in there," the airman offered. "You can watch it if you like."

The Marine shook his head. "Got to make a flight," he explained. "Got no time."

The airman shrugged and turned away.

"Thanks anyhow."

The airman was already gone.

Dear God, the Marine uttered silently, *if you're really around. Please don't allow that beautiful bird to die.*

Slinging his flight bag over his shoulder, walking off, the Marine made up his mind.

If *Titan* had to die, he'd be damned if he was going to watch. There are some things that are simply too sad, too terrible to have to see.

The old man wouldn't move away from the television set. He sat there listening, watching every bit of information, focused on what was happening. He looked like a bird stalking a worm. It was as if any word, any picture having to do with the situation of the *Titan* would be pounced on, digested, and then the vigil would start all over again.

"Would you like some lunch, Mister Langenberg?" asked the nurse.

He didn't answer. He didn't even let on he'd heard. *"Would you like some lunch now?"*

He didn't answer.

"Mister Langenberg?" A tug on his nightshirt sleeve.

Finally, he responded. "When you get around to it," he said softly. "When you get around to it, I'll eat it."

He could be a crochety patient, but she liked him. Most everyone did. Generally cooperative, fairly even in his disposition except when he thought someone was trying to put something over on him.

He really loved his girl. They all did. As a matter of fact, there was a kind of pride at Oak Knoll House that the child of one of their long-term guests was an astronaut.

The nurse looked again at Mister Langenberg.

He was crying.

Ron Fisher took a deep breath. The air seemed reasonably untainted. For the moment, things were in good order.

The injured athlete appeared to be taking it easy after losing all that blood. The gash was severe but they could get him medical attention when they got down. Miss Carlson seemed to be doing well after complaining of chest pains. The other passengers—especially the novelist—had been a big help with the ballplayer. There'd been enough room for everyone, even if there was damned little of it.

Nonetheless he knew that things were shaky. One bit of bad news, a peculiar sound, a puff of smoke, and everything would be up for grabs again. He understood how his badly frightened passengers, controlled for the most part on the outside, could still break and do dumb things, dangerous things, make fools out of themselves.

People worked that way.

Most of them, confronted with danger, would act like craven cowards, doing any abject, rotten thing to save their precious behinds. On the other hand, such pressure could also bring out—just as irresistibly—a certain amount of heroism.

Ron hoped there'd be no need—no need for either kind of behavior.

6

THE flight deck of the spacecraft was the center of fast-moving events. John Tillinghost was there with the two pilots. For the moment, all seemed to rest in their hands.

Pepper was sweating.

"There's no way we can bring this ship in with everybody jammed into that first-class compartment," he said.

"And if," added his second-in-command, "the environmental integrity of the first-class compartment goes, we have no place to move the rest of them."

"I know," responded designer Tillinghost. "I know that all too well."

"They'll rattle around like dry peas," Sager put in.

It was a tough conference—not at all comforting.

"So we need a lifeboat," Pepper stated. He exchanged a quick glance with Sager. It was obvious he was trying something on Tillinghost for size.

"A *lifeboat?*"

"That's right."

"Women and children into the lifeboats," Sager intoned solemnly like a purser organizing the deck of a stricken vessel.

The designer-engineer looked at one astronaut, then the other. His face, puzzled, offered scant encouragement.

"What are . . . are you . . . talking about?" he demanded.

"*Spacelab*," Pepper answered him. "We're talking about *Spacelab*."

Tillinghost shook his head emphatically.

"It's out of the question."

"Why's that?" Sager challenged.

Tillinghost kept shaking his head from side to side.

"Why's it out of the question?" Sager persisted.

"It's crazy. That's why."

"This whole thing is crazy," the astronaut went on. "The perfect piece of hardware, the quintessential spacecraft goes flooey. That's a little crazy."

"Look, Tillinghost. *Spacelab*'s due to be relieved within days. They're scheduled to pull the whole business down," Pepper interjected. "Why can't *Atlantis* take them all home?"

"There's no room."

Pete Sager produced a folded sheet of paper and began unwrapping it.

"There's room," he said quietly, confidently. "We figured it out. Volumetrically, *Spacelab* is about sixty-five percent the size of the whole passenger module of this vehicle. It's only carrying three crewmen right now."

Tillinghost said nothing. He simply studied the drawings of *Spacelab VII*, the penciled notes the two pilots had drawn on it.

"They're not under . . . NASA jurisdiction. There's no way they can be ordered to do what you—"

"You think they'll have to order one spaceman to help another?" Sager interrupted. "You're a hell of a de-

106

signer, Tillinghost, but you don't know shit about the folks who fly these high-priced toys you put together."

"Air supply?"

"A little tight," Pepper admitted, looking at the notes they'd scribbled on the *Spacelab VII* specs. "But we figure if they can get *Atlantis* up in about forty-eight hours, it could work."

"That's presuming plenty."

"Presuming we're going to make it at all is presuming plenty," observed the spacecraft commander. "But she's on 32B, standing up!"

Tillinghost bit his lip—hard.

"So?" Sager never liked letting anyone wiggle around half-hooked. He wanted to set the barb or let the fish swim away. It had to be one or the other.

"It *might* work." Tillinghost squeezed out the words as if they hurt.

"After a visual inspection," Pepper followed up unhesitatingly, "if *Spacelab* finds our heat-resisting capability compromised, we could avoid risking the women and kids with a chancy reentry. At least we could salvage that."

There was a strange look on John Tillinghost's face. He nodded his head affirmatively.

Pepper grinned. Then he spoke to Sager who was one move ahead of him with his finger on the button.

"Would you like to get on the horn with friend Ian aboard our target—see if he's got any vacant bunks?"

"Absolutely, skipper."

"*Spacelab*, this is *Titan*. Over."

"Hello, *Titan*. Understand you're experiencing a spot of trouble."

"Understanding affirmative."

"Sorry to hear it."

107

The signal was a bit weak, slightly distorted, but adequate.

"*Spacelab*, we have a couple of requests concerning our scheduled rendezvous."

"Let's hear them. Over."

"First, we want visual inspection of our spacecraft. We're especially concerned with hull integrity and with the condition of the tiles around Main Number Three."

"We'll be happy to oblige, *Titan*."

"Second request."

"Let's hear it, *Titan*," prompted Stafford aboard *Spacelab*, responding to Sager's long hesitation.

"In the event we're badly damaged, we wonder if you might take aboard a few unscheduled guests."

There was another pause in the conversation.

"Say again, *Titan*."

"How about playing lifeboat?"

Aboard *Spacelab*, Commander Ian Stafford's blood seemed to turn to ice water.

"Please explain," he asked.

"We'd like you to take aboard some of our female complement, a couple of kids, if we can get the launch date of *Atlantis* moved up."

Even as the conversation proceeded, *Spacelab*'s crew, Ernst Montigny, from Luxembourg, and Henri Lubac, floated nearby, listening intently to the conversation.

"What say you, *Spacelab*?"

Stafford looked up at his colleagues. Both men nodded to signal their approval.

"Sounds reasonable, *Titan*—depending on our space limitations."

"We're talking twenty-one," came Sager's voice over the *Spacelab* speaker system.

The three European astronauts again traded looks.

"What say you now?" came Sager's voice again.

"Sounds a bit dicey," Stafford observed. "But let's see if we can work something out."

There was no question it would pose problems. First, how to supply breathable air to all. *Spacelab*, designed for a small crew, was not easily adaptable as a life support system for twenty-four people—especially if twenty-one of them are excited, burning extra oxygen because of anxiety, fear.

Once the rendezvous coordinates were exchanged, and additional data were given to *Spacelab*, *Titan* signed off.

Stafford spoke to Montigny and Lubac. "I appreciate that, gentlemen."

Lubac shrugged, something of an accomplishment at zero gravity. "What else could we do?"

Indeed, Stafford told himself. What else could they have possibly done?

He wondered if Judy would be aboard. Would she be one of the women and children placed in the "lifeboat"? He would suggest it. After all, his personnel should not have the responsibility of keeping the survivors in order—under control.

A picture of Judy formed in his mind.

Bright-eyed Judy, gaminlike, dark as an Indian princess, the very picture of vitality and life. She was smiling, standing there in the buff, challenging him.

On one level the whole thing had been a mistake, one of those crazy errors of judgment to which human beings are often prone. There was simply too much of a chasm between them, too much of a cultural variant that would keep them apart. Both should have seen it. There was too much in both backgrounds that would remain centrifugal, no matter what.

109

Yet there had been their child. There *was* their child. And there had come joy, discovery, wonder. There had been, at least for a time, a very beautiful relationship, one that had helped them both through some of life's rough spots, rough spots in their own individual pathways toward the stars.

"Ian, we'd better clean up some of the crystal experiments," suggested Montigny, bringing his commander back to the realities of the moment. "With a crowd in here, things have to be stowed."

"You're correct, Ernst. I'll attend to the experiments myself."

There was housekeeping to do. Somehow they had to get everything as shipshape as possible for an incredible chancy mission of mercy.

They'd set themselves up in Space Star's Executive Suite at the corporation's Washington, D.C., headquarters. The bar had been set up. If mourning were called for, there *had* to be a bar. A bank of three large-screen color television receivers had been turned on to keep them updated on what the major networks were reporting. In addition, they were on a direct line with Houston, with California, with the Cape.

There were three men in the well-appointed room and one of them was showily excited, pacing the deep blue carpet, waving his arms even as he spoke.

"Cost?" shouted Jack Locke. "Who wants to consider the damn cost? Why do we persist in talking cost at a desperate time like this?"

"Because it's of major importance," answered Joe Wollen, a graying younger member of the House Ways and Means Committee. "It's got to be considered sooner or later."

"Make it later, damn it. Later!"

"But factor it in," insisted the Congressman doggedly. "You've got to factor it in."

"You really think I give a shit what this is going to cost?"

The man from South Dakota shrugged.

"All I care about is whether it works!"

"Someone has to care what it costs," insisted Wollen.

The third man in the room, a distinguished, older gentleman who resembled a work of Roman statuary, added his own contribution. "Astronomical cost!" he marveled. "The costs will be unbelievably high!"

"You and your puns," Wollen cracked, shaking his head.

"Those are my folks up there—my parents," Locke shouted, still lunging back and forth across the rug. "That's my spacecraft up there, my livelihood! There are other people—passengers up there—and every single one of them represents an irreplaceable human being with incalculable dollar value!"

"You sound suddenly like a humanist!" commented Wollen.

"Since when is *Titan* yours, Jack?" demanded the elderly man. "David's not dead—yet."

The younger Locke winced. "A manner of speaking," he sought to explain.

"I hope you realize the federal government is not going to pick up the tab for the rescue operation," said Wollen.

"Like I said, you think I care who's going to . . . to—" Abruptly, Locke interrupted himself, cut his own verbal flow off in full stream. He stared intently at his companion. "What did you just say?"

111

"The government is not going to pay the overtime, the additional expenses on the second launch, for *Atlantis*."

"That's what I thought you said."

"Just so long as you got it straight."

"But they were going to have to pick up *Spacelab* anyway, ten days down the trail."

"And the government is not going to pay for all the experiments that *Spacelab* had to scratch."

"Who is?"

"Space Star."

There was silence for a second or two. It seemed, as it hung there, like a dreadfully long time.

"Why isn't the government going to . . . going to . . . to pay for the launch of *Atlantis*, the rescue flight?" Locke asked very slowly, deliberately, seeming to enunciate the words with extreme care. "Aren't there . . . Americans out there?"

"Some," said the older man.

"Why should the taxpayers have to—"

"To hell with the taxpayers!" Locke came back hard. "Screw your taxpayer, whoever he is," he shouted angrily. "You're always coming up with the damned taxpayer when you don't want to play. The only time we hear about the poor bastard is when we need a program. It's always then you trot him out as a device for documenting a refusal."

"Hey, wait a minute!" objected Wollen, leaping to his feet.

"He's a myth," insisted Locke, "this pathetic little taxpayer of yours."

"He's not mythical at all," said the older man, a distinguished member of the Senate. "And he's having a very difficult time meeting his obligations."

"Up yours!" Locke snarled. "Up yours, Senator!"

*   *   *

112

Jay Pepper was the classic flying captain as he made his announcement. His voice had just the right casual, totally-in-charge quality.

"Ladies and gentlemen. This is your spacecraft commander, Jay Pepper, speaking. We have just worked out a plan of action that will, we believe, contribute significantly to the safety of all those aboard."

There was a long pause. It was as if he were trying to let it sink in.

"Despite all that's taken place," he went on, "*Titan* is fully intact. There is no integral damage to the airframe."

One could hear the sighs of relief.

"As a precautionary move, however, we are going to deploy the passenger module from the spacecraft to conform with the original plan and to effect a rendezvous and docking with *Spacelab*."

It was an exciting revelation—one that sent shivers of excitement up and down the spines of most of those aboard.

"I never expected," Mary Fittipaldi began, "to be involv—"

"Shhhh!" cautioned her husband as the skipper went on.

"What we are going to request is that women and children wait aboard *Spacelab* until *Atlantis* comes up to fetch you."

For a moment there was shocked silence. Then a buzz of excited conversation swept through the first-class compartment.

"What you think?" Jay Pepper asked Pete Sager.

The copilot shrugged. "It's a calculated risk," he said to his commander. "They could go bananas; they could

113

go along. We'll just have to wait it all out and see where it leads, if anywhere."

"Well," said Pepper, as if he hadn't really heard. "Let's play our next card."

Like the mechanical armature in one of the old slot machines, one of those mechanical marvels reaching in with a claw to pick out a necklace, a bauble of some kind, the great 624-inch mechanical arm of the spacecraft picked up the cylindrical passenger module from the cargo bay of the shuttle and lifted it out and over.

"My God," cried out one of the passengers.

"Incredible!" cried someone else.

It all opened up before them: space—luminescent, glowing, lovely. It was a whole new and glorious world.

Below them they saw the planet. Or was it above? Did it even matter?

The startled occupants of *Titan* were momentarily distracted from their predicament. Odors, nausea, fear were all put aside or muted for a few moments as they stared out into the unspeakable beauty surrounding them, temporarily holding them prisoner.

The pain hit Margaret Carlson hard.

It had been one thing to get David, her nephew, to agree as consulting physician that she could handle the rigors and stresses of the journey, another to leave her ailments behind.

There was no doubt.

"Is there anything the matter?" asked the very observant Miss Langenberg.

"My bag," she gasped, pointing. "Pills."

"Are you sick?"

All she could do was nod.

114

7

Tyuratam, in the heart of the Soviet Union. A crowded meeting room.

Everything was being done carefully, prudently— true Russian style, played very close to the vest.

No one really wanted a collision with supervisors, with the movers and shakers of the Soviet space program. It had to be done with concerted action—a full public agreement between all cosmonauts.

"It will read like this," Victor Ulanov announced. He cleared his throat loudly and read from the document he held in his hands. They trembled slightly although his voice remained firm and sure.

"We undersigned members of the company of the cosmonauts bring to the attention of our superiors in the government that we stand willing and eager to assist our brother voyagers in space in any way our government or the American government considers helpful."

"In any other way as well," someone added heartily from the back of the crowded room.

Ulanov threw the other a look but made no spoken response.

115

"All our names will be placed on this document?" someone inquired.

"That is correct," replied the big Ukrainian cosmonaut who was running the meeting.

It was not a meeting that would have major impact in the West. Indeed, most of the people gathered in the stuffy room were confident their offer would get side-tracked somewhere, but it was important to them that it be made. There was, after all, a brotherhood between them, those who had shown willingness to leave the bonds of earth, if only for a short time. There was a true brotherhood. It was an authentic bonding of the human spirit.

"How do we know this will ever get through to our friends?" another cosmonaut put in.

"We don't," Ulanov responded with his usual honesty. "We can only hope that somehow—in one way or another—they'll know of our concern."

"Anyone set up an icon corner?" came another question, sounding a bit frivolous.

Someone else snickered.

"Maybe that's all there is," said Ulanov before he moved the question, collecting the votes for which he hoped. "Maybe that's all we can do, to face the icon corner like old-time Russians."

Ulanov got his vote—unanimously.

The time was T plus forty-seven.

At that moment Polikov's pen stopped writing, stopped taking notes on the behavior of his fellow passengers, notes for a book that was beginning to come together in his head.

There was no interruption of the ink supply, no physical malfunction to account for the cessation of the activity

116

that had contributed to his own personal calm since he'd gotten the injured baseball player soothed and his wound dressed.

The writing stopped because Polikov at that point came to terms with what he suspected the eventual outcome of the *Titan* flight would be.

We're not going to make it, he said to himself. *It makes no sense at all to take notes, to observe the activities of fellow passengers, if we're going to be destroyed, if the spaceship, the passengers, the notes, were all to drift, blackened refuse, forever in space.*

Polikov was not a cowardly individual. He was certainly no pessimist, either. He'd done his share of dangerous things and emerged relatively intact—body *and* spirit. Somehow, as he viewed it, it was difficult to be totally pessimistic and to be a writer, for, at the root of the author's craft, there's an act of sharing, a belief in the notion that one human being can sometimes accept a fix from another.

I want to share this experience, he said emphatically to himself. *It's important to share this . . . this feeling, the whole dimensions of this unsettling experience.* There was immense gratification in it. He felt great pride in the fact that people were calm, responding reasonably well to the needs of others.

It shouldn't surprise you!

There had been the time at Penn Station in New York City when the whole Eastern seaboard had been slammed by an unprecedented blizzard. The station had been bulging with people. No trains were going in or out; more and more commuters were flooding in. He would always remember the way people had pitched in, helped each other, looked out for each other.

117

There were all kinds of instances of such help on the highway, in time of natural disaster, in major fires.

What the hell! he said to himself.

The pen began to move again.

Somehow they'd pull through. Somehow they'd get the damned spaceship back on the ground and, even if he didn't make it, he ventured an act of faith. The notes would somehow survive and perhaps someone else could share his story.

Houston.

Chandler was damned upset. He said so.

"Why didn't we have this data sooner? This has got me pissed!"

"We thought we were okay. You know how it is." The section chief was sweating. You could see the beads of sweat all over his forehead, running down his face.

"The hell I do. All I know is that if they'd gone for AOA as scheduled, we'd have had the world's most fatal screwup!"

They were talking about the information—the solid data—that made it clear that a scheduled landing of *Titan* at White Sands would be a physical impossibility. The orbit, the amount of fuel available, and the condition of the spacecraft were all conspiring against the principal plan of action first developed at Mission Control. Edwards in California on the next pass, the original plan, was also out of the question.

"Where do we land 'em?"

"Mexico City on the third orbit."

"Mexico City?"

"That's right."

"Out of the question," called Lem Connors from his

side table. Connors was presidential representative at the ad hoc meeting. "Politically out of the question."

"Rather have a catastrophe?" demanded Chandler, not giving an inch.

There was something terribly irritating about having a civilian put his two cents in. It was especially so if he was a politically motivated civilian.

"Have we got enough room?" demanded Chandler.

"Runways are long enough we think, strong enough to take that fat bird of ours."

"Permission?"

"State Department's working on it."

"What about medical backup, crash crews?"

"They're all right," someone else put in.

"Ours," Chandler asserted sharply. "What we need is to fly in ours—*fast*. There's no way they're going to be able, these local folks, no matter how good they are, the kind of gases, the sort of fire they're going to have to face if *Titan* comes in real hard."

Of course, as usual, Chandler was right.

"Do we have a backup?" he demanded.

For an instant his committee seemed to draw a collective blank.

"Work on that," he ordered.

"Okay," said Bobby Winthrop, one of his principal aides.

"What about chase aircraft? The people at State had better clear that."

"Len," Connors broke in, face reddened with exasperation, "there's no country anywhere that's going to let us chase fighter aircraft over their turf. It just isn't done!"

119

"It's got to be done," insisted the big man. "I don't give a particular damn how they go about doing it."

Chandler was in charge—at least as far as the landing was concerned. Jay Pepper and Pete Sager were flying the spacecraft and at that point the mission and the lives of all aboard were totally in their capable hands. But once *Titan* got into its earth landing phase, a hell of a lot of the authority, to say nothing of the responsibility, would rest squarely on Chandler's broad shoulders.

He was good at what he was doing. Something about Chandler drove other men, inspired confidence. He could infect others with the kind of faith that moves mountains even when he personally didn't believe they had the chances of a snowball sizzling in the hot furnaces of hell.

That's where a good portion of things stood at that particular moment—with snowballs in hell.

It was a peculiar place to die, a beautiful dusk flooding the overhead windows of first class. The lights of Perth on the western coast of Australia came into view.

Margaret Carlson was struck with the beauty, even as her body informed her that this was her appointed place, her predetermined hour.

Yet it did go well with the other dimensions of her unconventional life. Perhaps it was proper that she die in such a place. She'd never allowed herself to settle for ordinary, for mundane, for safe, in all the precious days given her. Despite her plain wrapper, there'd been a great deal going on inside the package of humanity christened Margaret Carlson. She'd resisted doing things the safe way, the easy way the world expects.

The young girl, Langenberg, astronaut–stewardess, whatever she was called, was so wonderfully gentle, solicitous. She could see tiny beads of perspiration about to take flight weightlessly from her forehead. Margaret found herself becoming terribly, weirdly conscious of detail. She recalled a poem she'd learned in grade school years earlier.

It began, "I heard a fly buzz when I died." It had been written by another woman who danced to her own tune. Somehow she was too weary to recall the poet's name, more than the first line of the piece itself.

All she could recall was that the speaker in the poem, dying, had become aware of a fly, one of life's tiny, irritating details.

Margaret Carlson did her best to hold on.

There was less pain than she'd expected. There was a kind of lassitude, an all-over tiredness coupled with a wrenching sensation that recalled to mind the feeling of having a tooth pulled. It was something like that, only different.

She managed to mumble a few words to the dark-eyed girl who was hovering there, holding on to her firmly.

"I . . . I won't . . . be . . . be the . . . first, will I?"

"Please don't try to talk."

"Didn't some . . . some Russians die in space?"

"Please, Miss Carlson."

"Let me talk . . . long as I . . . can."

There was a flicker of the old anger, the feisty quality she'd been so proud of.

Death seemed to be taking his own sweet time, she noticed. She'd expected better. Death should have been a seducer. She'd expected him to come as a Valentino, whispering obscene suggestions in her ear.

A coldness came creeping up her body. She could scarcely feel her lower extremities. The compartment grew darker.

121

"Headhunters . . . didn't get . . . me," she muttered proudly to the girl.

"What?"

The young astronaut had big, brown eyes. They were wide with concern. There was a sort of Indian look about her.

"Borneo. I went there . . . to Borneo. They . . . they didn't . . . get me."

"I'm glad," the girl answered, not knowing what else to say.

"Would have made . . . made . . . stringy dinner for them."

She tried to laugh at her own line, but it was altogether too much of an effort.

The astronaut smiled gently.

Everything was slipping away. It reminded her of an egg-timer, an hourglass. She could all but count the fragments of sand, the minute pieces of her life slipping through, accelerating.

She wanted to wish the girl well, to tell all of them on *Titan* she hoped they'd make it, but she wasn't able to. She simply tried to smile and fell backwards into . . . into whatever it was.

There was an all-enveloping darkness, a whole spectrum of breathtaking colors, and then it began to get brighter and brighter, brighter by far than she'd ever seen it.

"Commander," came Judy Langenberg's voice quietly over the spacecraft's intercommunication system. "We've lost a passenger. Miss Carlson has died."

"Died? How?"

"Heart, I believe."

The Payload Specialist kept her voice low, but she had

little doubt that most of the passengers were aware of the unfortunate woman's passing. This wasn't death hidden in a hospital. This was death headon, at close quarters.

"Keep it . . . as subtle as possible," counseled Jay Pepper. "And keep her strapped down."

"Affirmative," Judy came back.

What did the smiling jackass think she was going to do, Judy challenged silently, *let poor Margaret Carlson float around her compartment like a piece of discarded trash?*

"At the moment, ladies and gentlemen, spaceship *Titan* is approaching Sydney, Australia, where it is nighttime. She is approximately 120 miles above the earth at this point in her orbit. Houston has still not informed us when and where she'll attempt a landing, although it's presumed it will be at the Northrup Flight Strip at White Sands Proving Ground in New Mexico."

The sincere features of the TV newsreader registered the same bland degree of concern that he'd have shown in reporting the loss of a basketball game by the Knicks.

"We will, however, keep you fully informed as new developments are reported to us."

Then the TV coverage returned to a discussion of the layout of the space shuttle's passenger module.

8

THEY met near EPCOT, Disney's world of the future.
The two of them would work it out face to face, eyeball
to eyeball. McGettigan had just flown in with his family
from the Coast. Oates helicoptered over from the
launch. The ball was now theirs to play. *Atlantis* stood
poised on 39B, but she'd not move ahead of scheduled
launch date without them, without their agreement.

It was to be a gloves-off, no-holds-barred wrestling
match. The hotel suite—posh in its stark, futuristic
mode—would in no way inhibit that. The two men had
battled for too long to let such details make any real
difference. Now and again they'd even managed to coop-
erate.

Oates outlined the requirement. He did it incisively,
in his most businesslike manner. Finally, he stopped
talking and looked across at the other man.

"What the hell you people think we are?" demanded
Graham McGettigan.

"Supermen," Tim Oates responded flatly, matter-of-
factly.

"You're crazy," the labor leader growled at him.
"Crazy as hell!"

"With the dough your rank and file is hauling in, you damn well ought to be supermen."

McGettigan grinned. "Stuff it!" he told his friend and adversary, spearing a fat olive from a small salad plate with a concentration that was in a peculiar way edifying.

"We got to get *Atlantis* off within forty-eight hours!" Oates announced abruptly.

"What'd you say?" McGettigan nearly choked, spitting the half-chewed olive out on the small plate.

"Forty-eight hours."

"You need a prayer," said the man from the Coast, shaking his large, bald head emphatically.

"Then maybe that's what we'd all better do. Those people on *Spacelab VII* won't last more than fifty-two or fifty-three hours."

McGettigan shook his head sadly.

"You lost 'em, Tim."

Oates just stared as the labor leader went on.

"Can you get that straight? You've lost the whole damn bunch of 'em. They got to be written off. If not now, then later. New York and London lost a whole shipful once. *They* managed to recover. They lost 'em over seventy-five years ago from a craft with a similar name. Timmy, whether you're willing to admit it or not, you've got *Spaceship Titanic* out there!"

Oates felt a shiver along the back of his neck. It seemed to run nearly the length of his spine. "Wash your damn mouth out!"

"Look, Timmy. You know as well as I do it's the gospel truth! You Space Star hotshots are supposed to be a damn sight more realistic than those red, white, and blue assholes working for NASA, aren't you?"

Oates nodded dumbly.

"Well, prove it! You know perfectly well you've lost a

125

shuttle, a crew, a lot of fat cats out there. ESA's lost their crew, too. They're gone—all of 'em! It's time to cut your losses and get away from the table!"

"You're weirdo if you think we can just give up, leave them hanging out there!"

"Like they say in the hospitals now," McGettigan came back, "take no extraordinary means!"

Oates shook his head stubbornly. "Can't give 'em up," he insisted.

"I'm realistic. You're the weirdo. The airlines lose two or three hundred passengers in a single crash. Who's going to be devastated, wiped out by . . . what's *Titan* carry? Fifty-four?"

Oates nodded.

"Christ Almighty! Heinz had more varieties than that and Ho-Jo and Baskin-Robbins must have nearly as many flavors each."

"The President wants 'em back alive."

"The President wants another Republican Senate. Don't mean he's gonna' get it!"

"What can you do for us, Graham?" challenged Oates, leaning forward earnestly.

"You got the keys to the Mint?"

"What?"

"That's about it. The keys to the Federal Mint!"

Oates, red-faced, features beginning to swell, just stared at him.

"Do you always have to be an arrogant bastard?" he demanded finally.

"It's gonna' cost you. That's all I'm saying. You think it was gonna' be cheap?"

Oates shook his head sadly. "No. I knew damned well that you people were going to make us jump through

126

hoops. If you were involved, there was no way to keep it from being expensive."

"Forty-eight hours is crazy. You got to admit that, Tim."

Oates shook his big head again. It was peculiar, thought McGettigan, how his jowls jounced as he did so.

"You think I don't know that?"

For several moments, both men simply sat. It was Oates who finally broke the impasse.

"Can we do it, Graham?"

There was a long pause.

"I don't know," admitted the labor representative, shaking his own large, bald head. "*If* we do it, it'll be a hell of an accomplishment to share someday with the great-grandchildren."

"Can we work together?"

McGettigan shrugged and replied in an uncharacteristic way. "If we can't, those poor bastards out there don't stand much of a chance, do they?"

Oates shook his head. "No. Guess they don't."

"I'll handle it, Judy," Ron Fisher had assured her. He understood how important it was for her to deliver the message. He also admired her. He recognized her as a truly gutsy person, a skilled professional, one of the finest he'd ever worked with.

So, as she'd done many times before—in ground simulation and on previous missions—Judy Langenberg once more made her way into the airlock and reached for the intercom.

"Commander," she said.

"Hello, Sunshine," Pete Sager answered.

Judy stated her business. "I'm not leaving," she

stated. There was little readable in her tone. There seemed no emotion in her voice.

"What's that?" asked Pepper, scowling.

"I'm not boarding *Spacelab*," she said again.

"Sorry about that," Pepper answered. "But you are." There was no doubt in the way he said it. He was sticking to his guns.

"I'm sorry," she insisted. "But I'm staying aboard *Titan*."

"That's an order," Pepper said, never taking his eyes from the instrumentation in front of him. "You go aboard the lifeboat to direct the women and kids."

"An inappropriate order," she corrected him.

"You're not to be—"

"I'll not set foot aboard Ian Stafford's spaceship. I've promised myself and him that I'd never set foot in Ian Stafford's home, his quarters."

Pepper finally looked up. "It's not his home."

"Yes, it is. Remember, I was married to the man. I know."

Pepper was suspicious. Could what she was saying be the whole reason? It was unimaginable that one of the most solidly trained members of the astronaut team, one of the hottest pilots in the program, was turning down a legitimate order. Or was it something else?

"I don't believe, Jay Pepper, that you, unless the proximate situation is truly life-threatening, can order me to do something that violates my conscience, that offends my own personal standards."

"That's a hell of a speech," Sager commented. In his own way, Sager was trying to help her out.

"This is life-threatening," Pepper replied.

"My going or not going doesn't threaten passenger

lives. Ron is a civilian—not one of us. And there are natural leaders among the passengers themselves."

"What about your life?"

"I'm a fully trained member of this crew."

It had become a classic showdown.

Jay Pepper, among men, especially resented being crossed. He demanded what he called "rational coopera-tion" from everyone with whom he dealt. On the other hand, he didn't like hard-nosing another member of the club—especially a woman. And, in a sense, he also rec-ognized that this woman was right in feeling that her refusal to board *Spacelab* in no way compromised her passengers' safety.

"All right," he said crossly. "We'll belay that order for the time being."

It wasn't total capitulation but Judy knew she'd wrung her price out of the confrontation. "Thanks," she said.

"Now get down there and get things organized for a very touchy transfer."

He said it harshly, without any of the almost over-polite manner he usually affected. Partly, it was his price for her successful defiance. But part of it, Judy realized, had to do with the prospect of the transfer itself.

The original mission plan had not taken into consider-ation the likelihood of passengers moving into the other spacecraft. Transfer in space was, as *Titan's* professional crew had come to realize, a tricky maneuver that re-quired discipline and training. It was one thing for astro-nauts to hook up the docking collar, to balance all the mechanical components, to pressurize the connecting passageway, and to move through from one spacecraft to another at zero gravity. It was something altogether dif-

129

ferent for a frightened amateur who's just discovered the problems of moving weightless.

Judy quickly did what she was told, floating and scrambling back toward her post.

Los Angeles.

The ambulance attendant tried to reassure her as they lifted her off the kitchen chair on which they'd carried her out. He was just a fuzz-faced kid, but compassionate.

"You're gonna' be fine," he said. "Fine. You'll make it in plenty of time."

She kept right on sobbing.

"Got any other kids?"

She nodded her head affirmatively. "Two," she managed between sobs.

"Who's with 'em?"

"My mother."

"Then you know, with kids already, that you're going to be all right. You been through it twice before."

Mary Fisher wasn't sobbing about her own pain or as a result of any misgivings about the delivery she was about to undergo. It was for her husband on the spaceship *Titan*.

Why had they picked him? Ron?

He hadn't needed the job. It was all a matter of prestige, part of the huge publicity hype whipped up by Space Star and that damn Ted Bassano.

"Just think," Ron exclaimed when he'd first heard about it. "Some lucky flight steward will get the chance to actually get into space."

"What do you mean?"

"Space Star's looking for a senior flight attendant to fly the first passenger shuttle and—"

"Not you!" she'd interrupted.

"Why the hell not?" he'd demanded.

Ron had a great deal of pride. He was fit, good-natured, handsome, something of a master psychologist. He had a tremendous pride in the fact that he was one of Pan Am's top men in the passenger cabin.

"Because it's dangerous."

He'd scoffed at her. "Dangerous?" he'd challenged. "What's so damned dangerous about it? It's no more dangerous than an L-1011 run to the Coast."

Then he'd launched into an impassioned lecture on how safe the space shuttle had been rendered, how all the redundant systems backed up each other. At that point she'd become aware that he was going to be the man selected, the one chosen to go.

"It's the safest flying machine ever devised," he'd bragged on that momentous day—the day his application to join *Titan*'s crew had been mailed.

Another contraction began to build.

She groaned.

"What's the matter?" the ambulance attendant asked. He was gripping her hand.

"What the hell . . . you think is . . . the matter?" she managed.

She knew she'd make it to the hospital. She knew, too, that the birth would be quick and relatively easy. She only wished she knew how Ron would come through his own ordeal, whatever was happening out there somewhere in space.

The siren screamed.

The red lights flashed and the contractions continued. Life was about to be conferred.

Dawn over Baja California.

Ian Stafford had them visually.

Titan closed in rapidly on *Spacelab*.

"There they are," he said aloud. "Poor chaps!"

Lubac was watching with him.

"We got a bead drawn on you," came Pete Sager's chalky voice over the radio. "Comment?"

"Good to have you with us, Peter," Stafford came back.

"Not so sure, myself," wisecracked the American astronaut. "Maybe after you look us over I'll be able to agree how nice it is to be here."

There was, as ever, a touch of gallows humor, but the same serious concern managed to underlie everything, to lurk in everyone's mind. Was *Titan* sound enough to put up with the stress of reentry?

Carefully, with great precision, *Titan* approached the rather clumsy collection of cylinders and tubes that comprised *Spacelab*, the newest and nearest Western approach to a permanent space station. Cautiously, applying just the right Vernier thrust to accomplish what was intended without using any more of their precious fuel than was absolutely necessary, Sager turned *Titan* before the anxious gaze of *Spacelab*'s crew. Slowly he rolled her before them.

"What's the verdict?" Sager's voice buzzed in Ian Stafford's ears once the lengthy maneuver was completed.

Spacelab's skipper took a long breath before answering. "There is damage," he reported.

"Give us a rundown," came another voice that Stafford recognized as that of Jay Pepper.

"You've got tiles missing in the area of Main Number Three, *Titan*."

"How many?"

"I'd venture about . . . thirty-five to forty in all."

132

There was what seemed a long pause.

"That's a little dicey," Pepper acknowledged.

Despite the comment, delivered in the expected laconic style, there was no telling just how dicey the missing tiles problem would turn out to be. No previous shuttle had come in with anything close to that number of tiles missing from a single area on its surface.

"Can you help us locate the missing bricks on our diagrams?" interrupted Jim Taggart's voice from Mission Control in Houston.

"Affirmative, Houston," answered Stafford. "I'll attempt to give you a detailed report."

"Shoot when you're ready."

With careful attention to detail, using a diagram he had there in *Spacelab*, he proceeded to pinpoint thirty-seven missing tiles and sixteen others that, one way or another, looked suspicious.

Even in these circumstances Jack Garson found it easy to be contemptuous of his companions. They were such sheep, docile and obedient.

What did it ever get you? he challenged them silently. *The world belongs to the strong—those tough enough to take what they want when they want it.*

Hadn't he proven that with his life, his career? The fools who consider the needs of others before they consider their own deserve to come in second. And in the race of life there are few real winners.

I'm a winner! Garson crowed inside. *A winner always!*

"I want the women in this compartment ready to move one at a time into the interlock on my instructions," said Fisher. "There'll be no need to hurry and there'll be no need to push."

133

It was a strange and curious thing as they prepared to line up in zero gravity. They bumped about, floating like World War II barrage balloons.

"Let me call out the names one more time. The following will go aboard *Spacelab*."

One by one, he called out the names, marking each with a number.

"Princess Constance."

"Present."

"Trina Tillinghost."

"Yes."

"Lenore Burton."

"Present"

"Essie Locke."

"Here."

"Mame Gill."

"Yo."

"Betsey Garson."

"I'm here."

"Missy Grace."

There was no answer.

"She's here," her mother called out.

"Missy Grace," the steward called again.

"Here," came a small voice.

"Donatha Grace."

"Here too."

"Liz Tanner."

"Present."

"Mary Lou Ball."

"Right here."

"Donna Hall."

"Present."

"Diane Sommers."

"I have a question."

"Ask it," said Ron Fisher.

"Is this the order we go in?"

"That's right."

"Why?"

"We don't have time to discuss it."

"Doesn't it have anything to do with—"

"Nancy Fessenden."

"Right here."

"Mary Fittipaldi."

"Present."

"I still want an answer," said Sommers.

"Janet diLeo."

"Here."

"Nancy Sprigg."

"Present."

"Cindy Brokius."

"Present."

"Jimmy Beiser."

"I'm here."

"Prince Ahmed."

"That's wrong," called a youthful male voice.

"That is indeed wrong," repeated a more mature male voice.

"What's the error?" asked Fisher.

"Ahmed is a man. He is not going aboard *Spacelab*."

It was the young Saudi prince himself speaking. His father added his own words to it.

"As his parent, I insist he stay with me," said the senior in his own words.

The steward hesitated. Perhaps he could have bucked the problem to the flight deck, to one of the pilots. On the other hand, there would be more room for the youth on *Titan* than in the crowded quarters of *Spacelab*. Twenty-one was the absolute maximum they could handle and the princeling was nearly as large as a man and would consume more than the minimum amount of oxygen.

"Ahmed will stay aboard," he said. "That will make eighteen to transfer."

There would be no real opportunity to say a proper goodbye.

There would be no privacy whatsoever. Those who'd spent years together, who measured the days of their lives against each other's days, were granted only minutes before being separated.

What would be the nature of this separation? The question beset all of them. Would their orbits whirl them to opposite poles of the earth in the twinkling of an eye? Would the two spacecraft stay close, whizzing around the earth in tandem? Or would the separation amount to life for one, death for the other?

There seemed to be time for questions—little time for answers.

"You'll be all right?" asked the Prince Consort of Luxembourg.

"A question or a promise?" she asked.

"Both."

Gently, she laughed. "You've always been one for making your words serve double duty."

"Words are expensive."

"I know."

"But I'll spend some."

"Do."

"I love you."

"Profligate."

"Surely that's not too many."

136

"I should say not. I'd like to hear that group of words again."

"I love you, Constance."

"And I love you."

"It's been . . . beautiful," he said.

She flushed. "Don't use the past tense," she insisted. "It *is* beautiful. It will continue that way."

"Please God."

She nodded and added her own sentiments. "Please God."

Oblivious of others all around them, above them, below them, disregarding what, under different circumstances, might have seemed a matter of poor taste, they kissed. It was a comfortable looking kiss. To the casual observer, it might have seemed lacking in ardor, fire. But that was merely the external aspect of it. There was a deep exchange in their physical contact that, were it measured in footcandles, would have made all the lights aboard *Titan* seem dim indeed.

"*Au voir*, my love!"

"Go with God."

There were other goodbyes, many of them rendered all the more poignant because of the presence of the unfortunate Miss Carlson, still strapped to her space couch, face covered by a taped-on towel.

Carl Fittipaldi held his wife close and kissed her with all the panache and passion of a classic screen lover.

"Carl," she objected, coming up once for air. "There are all sorts of people watching."

"I know. Think there's any scouts from Hollywood? Maybe they'll give us a contract. I'd like—"

"Shut up," she broke in. "Kiss me again!"

*   *   *

137

It was T plus one-hundred-twelve minutes and twenty-three seconds. Having completed one full orbit, they were over Africa for the second time, hurtling through space at a staggering 18,000 miles per hour and crossing a new time zone every four minutes.

The transference of the women would take place in an uncertain line of floating forms.

Without warning there came a rush of four men just as Ron Fisher cracked the door to the airlock.

"What the . . .?" he gasped as bodies set him spinning.

He found himself irresistibly propelled backward through the hatch. Behind him pressed a mass of arms and legs, torsoes and heads, a three-dimensional puzzle of humanity.

In the midst of all this was the unpleasant face of Jack Garson. Crazily, he appeared to be smiling. But Ron Fisher realized he still hadn't become accustomed to reading expressions upside down.

"We're getting off this damn ship!" Garson snarled.

"You can't," said Fisher, still bouncing off the bulkheads from the violence of the shove that had sent him reeling backward. "Only women will be allowed on *Spacelab*."

"The hell you say."

There was something in Garson's eyes, something that could be read clearly, topsy-turvy or not. It was a kind of desperation that Fisher was too intelligent to ignore or underestimate.

"Listen, Garson," he sought to reason with the man. "Please listen to me."

Garson shoved him again and he found himself flipping backward into the overhead, near the flight deck entryway.

Two of the other intruding passengers were closing the hatch behind themselves, keeping Judy Langenberg, Gill, and Fittipaldi from grabbing hold of them.

"Shut this damn steward up," snarled another passenger. "Get this operation going."

There were four of them—one of the baseball players, Tanner, the oilman, and the singer-songwriter with kinky black curls, Beiser.

"Which one is it, Fisher?" Garson demanded.

"Which is what?"

"The lever to get us into *Spacelab*."

"You can't do it," Fisher objected again. He *had* to deter them. There was no chance for *Titan* if they lost discipline.

"This one?" questioned the musician.

"That goes to the tourist section," Fisher said, wishing he could recall the words even as he uttered them. The more they knew, the greater chance they had of picking out the correct lever. He'd made a serious error.

"Look out there," Garson ordered the monkeylike baseball player, the man who'd previously scaled the cabin before the onset of weightlessness. "Tell me what you see."

The man peered out the port. "There she is!"

"There who is?"

"*Spacelab*."

Fisher gained back some of his composure.

"You've got to stop this," he tried again. "If we don't all pull together, we're lost."

Garson ignored him. "How close is *Spacelab*?"

"Could spit on her."

"Tell me when we've caught on," Garson ordered. "We got to maintain momentum, surprise."

139

"You're right," said Tanner. "We can't fool around. We got to gain control of *Spacelab*."

"You're all crazy!" Fisher objected.

Garson had zeroed in on the correct handle. His hands were just inches from it.

"You got to wait 'til he's all docked. He'll give us a signal. Then we can crack the hatch. Not before or we blow our—"

Fisher was slammed into the bulkhead. He bounced hard against it, giving his shoulder a wrench.

"When we want to hear from you, we'll ask," said Tanner, who had caught him with a sucker punch.

"We told you to shut up," added the rock star.

Fisher tried to break through to them nonetheless. He saw the danger of what was going on.

"I'm trying to tell you something you have to know," he pleaded, sweating heavily. He was not as thoroughly trained in space systems as the rest of the crew, but he understood very well what could happen. "It's im—"

"We're on," said the baseball catcher with his head up next to the port. "We're on. Did you feel that little jolt?"

Garson put his hand on the lever.

Fisher, from somewhere above him, gambled and made a lunge to pull him away from it.

Although he took the man by surprise, Garson had managed to get a firm grasp on the lever before Fisher touched him. The steward was trying to hook his arm under Garson's before he really got hold of the lever in order to pull him back away from it.

However, there was something about moving fast in zero gravity that subverted him. He didn't manage to get it right. Instead of pulling the man away, the force of his lunge, mistimed, assisted the little businessman in doing what he was simply preparing to do.

140

It was quick, violent, and final.

Like the action of some unimaginable vacuum cleaner, the airlock was scoured of its human contents, objects of any kind that weren't built in. Five helpless human beings were sucked, suitless, into the void.

They didn't even have time to scream!

9

On *Titan's* flight deck everything seemed to go haywire.

"What the . . .?" shouted Sager, as alarms sounded, red warning lights flared and flashed.

"What's happening?" demanded Pepper.

"Somebody blew the hatch!" Sager replied. He was thoroughly preoccupied, marshaling himself to take whatever precautions were available to him. He was checking everything. Training and instinct had jointly taken over—reflexes. When the alarm sounds, the super pilot is ready, not with heroics, but with solid, logical, preprogrammed action.

His hands seeming to blur with the speed at which they moved, he went through the whole drill, one step after another. He checked everything out, worked all the backups.

"Somebody's out there!" Pepper shouted, his voice sounding shrill and strange.

The unthinkable was happening.

"Nothing I can do," Sager said grimly between set teeth, not responding at all to the chilling words of the spacecraft commander.

142

"More than one!" Pepper cried.

"Check the cabin," he said.

"First-class compartment," Pepper said. "This is flight deck."

"I think we just lost Ron," came Judy Langenberg's voice.

"Shit!" said Sager. All he could do would be to dock with *Spacelab* and repressurize.

"*Titan*, what's your status?" came Taggart's voice from Houston. He was apparently reacting to telemetry indicating some sort of anomaly aboard.

"Mayday!" someone called from *Spacelab*. "Bodies overboard!"

For agonizing seconds Sager had a terrible feeling they might have lost the whole passenger component. Yet he'd just heard Judy's voice.

Somehow he had to check again.

"Ron," he said into the intercom mike. "Ron, are you there?"

He heard Judy's voice again, clear and strong at this point.

"Ron's gone," she said grimly. "He and four passengers were sucked out of the airlock."

"Oh my God," said Pepper, a strange look in his eyes.

"Come in, *Titan*," Taggart was simultaneously insisting from the ground.

"Tune him out," Sager snapped, seeming unmindful of just who was in command.

"Will do," Pepper acknowledged, forgetting protocol himself, flipping all the switches, cutting out the backup systems this time as well as the principal speaker.

What the hell had happened?

143

It took several seconds to get his bearings, to realize what had happened—where he was.

Ron Fisher knew he had had it. He was in open space, no suit, no protection. He was about to die. It would be minutes, but he'd lose consciousness in sixty more seconds or so.

The realization of all this, quickly coming to terms with it, was his last fully lucid thought. He knew capillaries were popping all over him, lungs, air passages, deep inside his brain.

Before, he'd imagined it'd be like swimming, working arms and legs against the water to propel oneself from spot to spot. *But I got no bathing suit!* This was weird. There was nothing here, nothing to work against. Empty. Totally empty. Only that damn ballplayer and— Who were the others?

What the hell did it matter?

He was floating farther and farther from the spacecraft, still affected by the violent suction that had drawn him out. He tried to wonder about the physics of it, but it was hard to string his thoughts together.

He was light-headed, gasping wildly for breath—the breath that wouldn't come. There was nothing at all to inhale. He was on instinct—reflex. There had to be air. The sun blistered his flesh cruelly, roasting him.

Why doesn't somebody put up a damn beach umbrella?

He tried to think of Mary . . . in California, of his mother . . . where was she? But it was hard to focus on anything. He did manage for a second to visualize Mary—

There was a red mist in front of his eyes. He didn't realize his nasal passages and his throat were hemorrhaging badly.

144

His own name ran wildly, crazily, through his head like a drug-maddened vandal running amuck in an abandoned schoolhouse. *Ron Fisher! Ron Fisher! Ronnie Fisher! Ronnie Fisher! Ronnie Fishbait! Ronnie Fishkill! Fishill! Fiskar! Fishcart! Fichter! Fisser! Fisser! Pisser! Misser! F-F-Fisser!*

He didn't realize much of anything as he sucked instinctively, vainly trying to get something to breathe. There was only the aureole of blood droplets. They offered him nothing he could use.

The pain was bearable.

Ronnie! Ronnie! Ron! Ronnie! Other name . . . hard . . . too hard . . . Ron! Ro–o–o . . .

His last thought might well have been Mary, the new baby, had his bleeding brain been able to manage.

He lost consciousness altogether.

Sager flew *Titan* with its passenger module above it on the end of its crane just a few feet from *Spacelab*'s docking collar.

The form of a man floated between the two spacecraft. It took only a glance to determine whose form it actually was. From the Space Star coveralls there could be no doubt whatsoever.

"Any chance he's alive?" Sager demanded.

"No way," Pepper came back, shaking his head.

"Three to four minutes?"

"Used two already."

"Conscious?"

"Uh-uh."

"*Titan*, what's going on?" called Houston on yet another backup system Pepper'd overlooked.

Neither pilot seemed to hear.

145

"Body's blocking us," said Pepper, looking again at the television monitor. There was an edge in his tone.

"Don't sweat it," Sager responded, maintaining an awesome degree of concentration.

"Push it out of the way."

Sager said nothing. He simply continued to fly the spacecraft.

"Nudge it out of there."

Sager still didn't look up, but he spoke. "Shut up, Jay."

"What'd you say?"

"Relieve me if you want to. Fly this sucker if you like. But in the meantime, shut the hell up!"

"You think you can get these two bastards together with . . . with . . . a stiff in there?"

"I'm taking him aboard."

"What?"

"You heard the man," he said. Then he talked half to himself, half to an imaginary audience. "Step right up, ladies and gentlemen. See the space weirdo who'll put the body in the ring and dock the spaceships at one and the same time."

"You can't do that."

"Watch me, babe. Just watch!"

It was a careful, precise business. Turning the whole operation into a strictly manual one, Pete Sager flew the ungainly passenger module closer to the other vehicle, governing with incredible delicacy the Vernier jets that controlled the roll, pitch, and yaw of the whole expanded vehicle.

"What the hell are you doing?" Pepper demanded.

"You said nudge," Sager answered, still focused on the task. "So I'm gonna' nudge."

"All right. Get him out of there."

146

"I'm gonna' nudge him in, not out."

"What?"

"Into the docking collar—the airlock."

For a moment, Pepper might have objected, might have made his second-in-command relinquish the difficult, exacting, and perhaps dangerous project of catching hold of a free floating corpse and docking a space vehicle in a single operation.

Pepper, however, knew Sager too well to say anything more. For several seconds he sat silent. Finally, he did speak, but his words were more supportive than critical.

"Don't screw up, Pete!"

"Not a damn chance," Sager answered, playing the controls of *Titan* with the body English of a Pac-Man addict.

There was no warning.

The woman began to scream. She screamed no words, nothing coherent. It was raw sound.

Then it became clear what had set her off, what she was dealing with.

At the viewing port of the compartment, no more than four feet from where she floated, the frozen corpse of Jack Garson, her husband, stared at her, eyes distended, ruptured, bloodied. He floated there like a dead, somewhat bloated fish, head surrounded by a bubble of red mist, crimson droplets.

"Oh God!" someone exclaimed in disgust.

The woman continued to scream and moan as she stared at the terrible vision of the man she'd lived with.

"Easy, Mrs. Garson," Judy Langenberg said, trying to make her way through the crowded compartment to comfort the hysterical woman.

147

"Cover that damn port!" Senator Gill shouted. "Use a shirt of some kind, a jacket, anything."

"There's a shade—optical," Judy volunteered as she took Mrs. Garson in her arms.

Another corpse floated past—unrecognizable—facing away from *Titan,* arms raised in place like an awkward imitation of Superman's flight technique.

"Jesus God!" someone shouted. "There's another one."

"There's no need to panic," Judy called to the very shaken people. "The pressurization hasn't failed. The accident was caused by those who didn't follow instructions."

"Can it happen again?" someone asked in a teary, trembling voice.

Judy decided it was time for tough, absolutely direct answers.

"Yes," she said flatly. "It can happen if someone panics and fails to do what he or she is told to do. We can make it with discipline if we take advantage of the training and skill of the crew, the dependability of the hardware and its backup systems."

"You being honest with us?" came a male voice.

"Whether we make it or not," Judy answered, "will be governed in large part by our actions. On that, I'm being totally honest."

Things got markedly quieter. The sobbing seemed to abate. The bodies weren't in easy view of the passengers. The mood seemed to be changing.

"The order of departure remains the same," Judy said. "We'll wait for word from the flight deck."

Judy Langenberg was not alone in seeking to restore order. A number of passengers had freely joined in. Gill and his wife had become major sources of reassurance.

148

Tillinghost quietly explained things to those willing or able to listen. Fittipaldi and Polikov had already proven themselves towers of strength. The royal couple from Luxembourg were also strongly supportive as was the Saudi Prince. Others were playing cards, whistling tunes, suspending cameras and pencils in zero gravity, and acting oblivious of the danger.

Things were settling down in the passenger compartment.

T plus one-hundred-thirty-eight minutes and three seconds, over the Indian Ocean.

"We have a solid linkup," Pete Sager finally announced to his commander.

"Houston," Pepper said. "We have achieved docking."

"I'm ready to pressurize," Sager reported to his command pilot.

"Do it."

"Any problems?" Houston asked. "We've lost docking telemetry."

"Nothing we couldn't take care of."

"What was that Mayday?"

"Don't mean a thing. False alarm."

"*False alarm?*"

"Affirmative."

There was a long pause. Both pilots could picture Taggart trying to digest all he'd been hearing.

"We were beginning to wonder when we didn't hear from you," he finally said.

"Aren't you going to tell 'em?" Sager mouthed softly, lifting his throat mike off his neck.

Pepper shook his head.

"Are you pressurized?"

"Affirmative."

"What's this about repressurization?" demanded the Cap-Com from Houston.

Pepper hated to report the news. His judgment, however, overcame his reluctance. Only his tone of voice gave it away. There was a kind of distancing in his tone— a kind of emotional alienation.

"Houston, we had trouble in the earliest part of the docking procedure—casualties."

"We copy, *Titan*."

"Several passengers blew the hatch prematurely and were lost."

Chandler's heavy voice broke in. "Pepper, what the hell were passengers doing with hatches?"

Pepper grimaced as he answered. "They forced the steward into the airlock and blew the hatch."

"God!" came Chandler's spontaneous exclamation.

"How many casualties?" asked Taggart.

Pepper was unguarded at this point, not bothering to inquire about the security of the channel.

"We lost the steward and four passengers. Do you want names?"

"That's negative," said Taggart, apparently responding to instructions being passed to him at the Space Center.

"But you *do* understand the identity," Pepper began, "of . . . of . . . the lost crew member?"

"You did say steward?"

"Affirmative."

There was a pause. "We copy, *Titan*."

Then, there was silence.

"Well, I did it," Pepper said angrily.

"Wasn't the most pleasant duty of the day, was it,

Jay?" Sager commented with considerable sympathy for his colleague.

Pepper bit his lip and shook his head. "Sure as hell wasn't."

Langenberg despised doing it.

She and Fisher had become good buddies. During the training for the *Titan* flight, they'd spent a lot of time together. Some of the NASA and Space Star types had resented the fact that Fisher was a commercial airline purser making a lot more money than they did for similar work. Perhaps, too, he was a little formal for many of them, tried too hard to be liked. Thus, they had little time for him; let him go almost everything alone.

Langenberg couldn't operate that way. She answered the redhead's questions, gave advice, saw to it that Fisher was always included in things.

Dragging herself, Langenberg entered the airlock, resolving to place Ron's body in the by then contaminated, totally deserted tourist compartment.

"Ron!" she called sharply.

There was, of course, no reply.

"How'd you let it happen, Ron?" she called out even louder. Reaching out, she shook Fisher's shoulder, being careful not to push the body too hard and lose control of it in the zero gravity of the empty airlock.

Fisher's remains simply floated against a bulkhead, head lolling backward, the mucous membrane of his face bright crimson. There was still an aureole of blood droplets around him. His flesh was badly burned from the sun, much discoloration in evidence. Actually, Langenberg knew he was cooked—thoroughly broiled in his own juices.

151

"I'm sorry, Ron!"

Then regretfully, gently, she tugged at the carcass that had just recently contained the personality of her friend and colleague and tugged him into the tourist compartment, working quickly to minimize the amount of fumes that escaped into the airlock atmosphere. Things were bad enough on *Titan*.

There was no way they could let a body just float in plain view in an airlock through which all the women and children would have to pass to board *Spacelab*.

Ron's corpse seemed reluctant to go.

At one point, after she managed to get the hatch open, the dead man's leg seemed to catch in the hatch mechanism. Langenberg had to rip away a piece of material from Fisher's Space Star coveralls to get him through.

Until *Spacelabs VI* and *VII*, the European Space Agency's laboratories had been used merely as satellite elements, always attached to the shuttle. With the development of *Spacelabs VI* through *XII* they were independently orbiting systems with their own airlocks and oxygen supplies.

Although the whole assembly still had to fit in the sixty-foot limitation of *Atlantis*'s cargo bay for deployment and retrieval, the space shuttle's sophisticated progeny could sustain itself adequately for limited periods of time.

She would not prove luxurious or even marginally comfortable for the space refugees, but she would surely be preferred to dying.

"They're on their way up to you," came Judy Langenberg's well-remembered voice, piped over *Titan*'s communications system.

"We welcome our visitors," Ian Stafford came back.

Hearing Judy's voice gave him a peculiar feeling. He wanted to add a personal message, some acknowledgment of her. He did nothing, however.

Lubac opened the hatch and helped the first fugitive aboard.

"*Bienvenue!*"

"Thank you."

The words of welcome seemed sincere enough, but the luxury was clearly gone. As a matter of fact, *Spacelab VII* resembled a stainless steel diner with counters, shelves, closed metal cabinets extending all along the corridorlike compartment.

"Please move away from the entry, ladies!" Ian Stafford called out to his new charges. "Let's afford room for the newcomers."

"Are you the English astronaut?" one of the women asked.

"Ian Stafford at your service," he said.

"Thank you for taking us aboard," said a striking looking woman with silver hair. "I'm Mame Gill." She floated toward him with her hand extended.

Ian Stafford took her hand.

"Please find a place to hold yourself up or down," Lubac was telling them as they entered *Spacelab*. "The sooner you can find a comfortable spot, the sooner we can let *Titan* tend to her wounds."

"We've used up a hell of a lot of fuel," Pepper observed.

"Unavoidable," said Sager.

"Except for that extra business of getting Fisher aboard."

"It didn't make that much difference, Jay. I had to get

153

him away from the docking collar in one direction or another. All that rocking and pitching and yawing was going to cost us some fuel one way or another."

Pepper grunted.

In a sense it was relieving to have lightened their burden to the tune of eighteen souls. As a matter of fact, with the death of Miss Carlson, the five lost overboard, and the eighteen who boarded *Spacelab*, there were twenty-four of those who had originally boarded *Titan* whose fate had been sealed or otherwise directed away from the responsibility of Jay Pepper and his second-in-command.

"We gonna' make it, Jay?" Sager asked.

The commander merely grunted again.

Actually Sager wondered why he'd asked. It was a dumb question. Of course they'd make it. They had the crew, the spacecraft. Only lesser men could screw up!

Back at Kennedy Space Center in Florida.

Ted Bassano, despite his title with Space Star and his undergraduate degree in science, wasn't altogether sure what was happening.

"The damn press are on us like bugs on a piece of meat."

"That's what you're for," said the man opposite him.

"Need help," Bassano confessed.

"Never thought I'd hear you admit it."

"Explain it to me."

The man sitting opposite Bassano was Bobby O'Neill, former member of the space shuttle team, now a senior consultant for a West Coast thinktank.

"It's not too complicated," O'Neill responded. "With the shutdown of engine three somewhere along the line, the spacecraft's got just barely enough thrust to take her

154

out of orbit on a shallow reentry glide and no cross range. Unless they wait a day they can ditch it in Mexico on the third orbit."

"That's not what we wanted them to do," Bassano pointed out.

"What's even more alarming is that there's a deteriorating environment aboard—how badly we can't tell—as fumes from the burnt-out engine have somehow managed to find their way into the passenger compartment. A third complicating factor may involve the loosening of some of the heat shielding tiles around engine three."

"How many?"

"Nobody's talking. But if there are too many," O'Neill went on, "there could be a hell of a barbecue in the sky before the day is out."

"That bad?" asked the PR man.

"That bad!"

Los Angeles at dawn. To a group of amateur astronomers peering through field glasses and miniature telescopes, *Titan* was visible, streaking across the southern sky, almost at the end of its second orbit.

The delivery was easy—by the book.

The mother came through in excellent condition and was mildly sedated after seeing the child. Ron and Mary Fisher's child, Peter Langenberg Fisher, was born at T plus one hundred eighty two minutes in the mission of the space shuttle *Titan*, a mission he'd grow up to remember.

He had red hair, just like his father's.

10

On the ground, Houston Control continued to work with a kind of determination that, for all its single-minded intensity, seemed to all but the most astute observer totally routine.

For all of that, however, there was strain. It was the strain of impotence, leaving "can do" men realizing there was nothing whatever they could do to affect the outcome of the mission. They had come to realize that true command decisions must originate from the flight deck of *Titan*.

The Mission Director and the Cap-Com, almost without knowing it, drifted into their deferred conversation.

"Do you blame me?" demanded an exasperated, frustrated, deeply shaken Jim Taggart, "for wanting to bail out of this crazy rat race?"

Chandler looked over at the younger man almost contemptuously. "You can't get out of it."

"What?"

"There's no way."

"I can hand in my resignation and head for the door. It's been done before."

"None of us can—particularly those your age, those

156

with your level of training and scientific expertise." Then Chandler, the old jet-jockey astronaut whom Taggart and others like him often thought of as an unfeeling, unthinking macho man of the heavens, astounded him.

"We're packing to leave," Chandler said. "Crazy and confused as all this may be, it's part of something that can't be changed or cut back on for long. There was a time when mankind didn't want to leave the cave. There was a time when we didn't want to go over those hills that crowded the horizon. One way or another, man is leaving this used up, screwed up planet. Whether he gets trigger-happy and blows himself out of it or whether he manages to keep his cool a little longer and moves off about sixty or seventy years down the road, he's going. That, my young friend, is what this is all about!"

It's the English Commander of *Spacelab*.

"Houston, this is *Spacelab VII*."

"Roger, *Spacelab*. We read you."

"I have all our visitors aboard. We've lost visual contact with *Titan*. The passenger module is back inside the cargo bay. We observed as she pulled away that two or three additional tiles have worked themselves loose."

"Damn!" said Chandler from behind the Cap-Com's seat. "Can you locate them for us?"

"Immediately below the area we reported to you before."

"Lower?"

"Affirmative, Houston."

"We copy. Thank you kindly, *Spacelab VII*."

"Sorry it couldn't have been better news. Over and out."

Chandler shook his head. Both he and Taggart knew it

157

all too well. Whatever happened, it was going to be dicey—real, honest-to-God dicey!

Spacelab.

There was no way to get any of the remaining scientific work accomplished. *Spacelab VII* had been totally thrown out of operation as an experimental enterprise. With the pressurized compartments of the system jammed with people, on bulkheads and overhead as well as on the deck, all previously scheduled experimentation, except for a couple of radio-ranging processes and some agricultural and chemical work already deployed outside, had been canceled.

There was little to do but wait.

Mame Gill carefully moved herself into a properly aligned position in gravitational terms to talk to Ian Stafford, even if there was no true gravity around. Mame found it difficult, disturbing, to talk on a different plane or to speak to someone upside down or sideways.

"Do you have a moment?" she asked.

"Quite a few, as a matter of fact."

"Just promise me you won't float away when I'm in the middle of my question."

"I promise."

Mame was looking for a professional opinion.

"How does it look to you?" she asked.

"How does what look?"

"Titan's prospects."

There could be little beating around the bush when Mame Gill asked questions. She had a way of transfixing one with her bright blue eyes.

"If the . . . the rest of the tiles hold, things should be all right."

"The rest?"

158

She was quick. He had suspected she might be.

"Some are missing."

"How many?"

"Couple dozen."

She shook her head. "Surely you were trained to be more precise than that, Commander Stafford," she said. She made him feel like a young student being chastised by his teacher.

Ian Stafford found himself flushing. He always did so when someone challenged him. It ran in the family.

"Forty-one," he said.

"Forty-one?"

He nodded affirmatively. He didn't like telling her, but it was difficult to avoid it. She was a tough, insistent woman. Somehow, too, he was very much aware of who she was. There was a measure of reverence involved.

"That's a lot," she said. She seemed somber as she made the statement.

"Yes. It is."

"Too many?"

"Don't really know."

"What kind of answer's that?" she demanded. For a few seconds she seemed to flare up.

"An honest one," he answered. "They don't know how many is too many."

"What did Houston say?"

"They were noncommittal," he answered honestly. "They shared our concern, but they didn't volunteer much except to say it'd be dicey."

She nodded agreement. "What happens if . . ." She stopped herself. "But I know the answer to that, don't I? It almost happened to him the first time . . . aboard *Mercury*."

She was talking about her husband's first orbital flight.

159

It had brought real anxiety, genuine fear to the space program.

Stafford said nothing. There was nothing appropriate to add. She clearly understood what was going on. She had things figured out jolly well. Although she probably didn't know the shuttlecraft in great detail, she'd likely heard all the gory implications if too much heat built up during reentry. She'd likely heard all the horror stories.

"We have to . . . to presume that . . . Pepper and Sager have . . ."

"I know what they're supposed to have," she said. "I know they probably have it, too. There is, however, the problem of the machine itself."

"That's correct," Stafford agreed. "There is clearly that."

He wasn't going to kid her. He wasn't going to try. She'd likely see right through any such attempt.

"What about *this* affair?" She circled her hand to indicate the other refugees seated everywhere.

"Good shape," he said jauntily.

"You really believe that, don't you?"

"I do."

"Will the air supply be adequate?"

"If everyone holds themselves under strict emotional control."

She looked at him, a question in her eyes. "Why's that important?"

"If people don't get panicky, start screaming, we'll be all right. When they get too excited they use up oxygen. We won't have that much to spare."

"But it will be dicey," she said, borrowing NASA's word. Or was it Stafford's word?

He nodded.

"Dicey, indeed."

*　　*　　*

160

Judy, with little to do for the moment, huddled in a corner of the first-class compartment, reviewing her life.

There was little to be totally satisfied with. She had made the NASA team. She had built up an enviable record as a pilot. She had given birth to a lovely human being, Karen, a child she dearly loved.

But there had been failures, false starts. She had made wrong-headed decisions. There had been many more of them than she could ever feel comfortable with.

The greatest source of dissatisfaction was her failure to accomplish the big deed. As an ambitious girl, one who could never cheerfully accept the limitations imposed on her sex, she had always been determined to do what her father called "the big deed."

"You all right?" asked Carl Fittipaldi.

"I'm fine," she said.

There was something about being idle—about being deprived of any real opportunity to control her fate—that tempted Judy to wonder about something that never would have crossed her mind had she been on the flight deck with a job to do.

She could visualize Death in her mind's eye. He was slick and handsome, the classic seducer. He stood out there ahead of them, checking his watch, whistling between his teeth.

"You got a family?" Fittipaldi asked her.

"A daughter."

"How old?"

"Seven."

"She's got a hell of a mother."

"Thanks."

He was a good man, this mechanic or whatever he was. He'd shown more character, more leadership in the crisis than most of those who would have considered themselves his betters.

"You were pretty terrific yourself," she said.

"I was scared shitless," he admitted.

"You weren't alone," she pointed out. She laughed. Somehow he made her feel better. Death seemed to recede—disappear.

Washington.

The burly man seemed planted behind the broad jousting ground of desk. He leaned forward, resting much of his considerable weight on his knuckles. He studied the reports spread before him. Even the top of his head, all one could see of it, looked serious.

There were about a half-dozen others in the room. They were important men, accustomed to running things, accustomed to calling the shots as they saw them. In this instance, however, they were vassals waiting on the big man's words, his reaction to the calamitous situation spread before him.

Like children, they sat silently awaiting some reaction from the parental authority on the far side of the desk.

Finally the President looked up from the reports and advisories, the new bulletins from the spacecraft.

His natural flush remained but some of the color had drained from his face. He seemed very tight around the mouth, the flesh yellowish, almost gray. He also seemed to have a little difficulty controlling his speech. It was thick with emotion.

"I . . . I think, gentlemen . . . we have to develop a new position in the . . . the light of . . . all that's happened, is happening, is . . . about to take place."

No one said anything. There was nothing to say.

162

"I think we . . . have to . . . to write them off," he concluded, with a noticeable tremor.

There could be no doubt in any mind. The Chief Executive was deeply upset. It wasn't the first time that heavy tidings had impacted on the Oval Office. It wasn't the first that American objectives had gone awry. But somehow the imminent loss of the shuttle *Titan* struck especially hard at this President. It had been his notion that the space shuttle be developed commercially to compensate the nation for at least a portion of the staggering development costs. It had been at his insistence that the commercial license for the passenger-carrying spacecraft had gone to Space Star. It had been at his executive urging that things had been pushed along hurriedly.

"How can we . . . write it off?" someone challenged. It was the deputy head of the Space Agency.

"We . . . we have to be . . . prepared," the President responded. He said it gently, seeming to modify somewhat the finality with which he'd used the phrase "write it off."

"We are prepared. We have been prepared," said the official, defending his agency like a mother bear defending her cub.

"I mean," explained the President, "we have to be . . . braced for . . . a total loss."

"We're not giving up," insisted the deputy. "Not at NASA we aren't."

"It's not a matter of giving up," the big man behind the desk came back. "It's a matter of developing a backup position."

"Space Star doesn't back up," suggested someone else.

163

"Gentlemen!" insisted the President. "I'll not have bickering. We have no backup position. We have no notion of how to handle this if *Titan* is lost because we never imagined the damn thing would go haywire on us."

Clearly the President had put his finger on it. Never had they believed it would fail. The American space effort had gone well from its very beginnings. There'd been a scattering of losses and setbacks: the tragic deaths of Grissom, White, and Chafee; the near-miss with *Apollo XIII;* a scattering of lesser problems—hardware blowing up, glitches here and there—extracting their own price. But, by and large, things had gone so well that all concerned had fallen victim to the expectation of success every time a spacecraft lifted off. Surely no one in his wildest dreams had expected so great a potential loss to become a probability.

The usually silent Vice President spoke. "What are the true odds?" he asked.

"It's not a crap game," the NASA deputy came back.

"At best the odds are lousy," the President responded.

11

ELLINGTON Air Force Base near Houston.

Loneliness could be a pain in the ass!

Major Rick Gill had never made allowances for loneliness. In all the earlier years of his life it had never been a factor. He'd been surrounded by friends and family—supportive, loving people. He'd never been forced even to consider going it alone.

The electric alarm clock on the nightstand next to his narrow bed made ridiculous whirring, gurgling noises. At least the damn thing had the tastefulness not to tick. The last thing he needed was the sound of a ticking clock.

Once or twice in previous years he'd wondered what it might be like existing at the BOQ, being responsible for his own entertainment, setting his own schedule for off-duty hours, sleeping alone at night. But it had been idle conjecture back then, having little urgency or significance.

He chuckled aloud, a cynical chuckle.

Crazy, uncontrollable things had conspired against him . . . then. His own stupid, sexist lack of consideration, his own tendency to say too much of what he felt every time something bothered him. On the other hand, there was Sally's hair-trigger temper. There was her damn stiff-necked New England pride. There was her insistence about the . . . the apppointment to the shuttle program. That was the real joker in the deck. What the hell was so much worse about being married to an astronaut? She was already hitched to a jet-jockey! Why was it that the two of them—

The telephone bell startled him.

The hell with it!

It rang again.

He hesitated. Lonely or not, telephones were damned unreasonable.

A third ring.

Finally he gave in.

"Major Rick Gill here."

"Pat, I got bummer news! The shuttle's got problems!"

Colonel Bobby Clancy had never been one to beat around the proverbial bush. Bobby'd let you have it full load, both barrels.

"What you mean?"

"They're doing—far as we've heard—a once-around abort. Seems there's a major malfunction in one of the engines. There's also talk about gas leakage into the passenger module."

"Shit! My folks are on it."

"I know. That's why I called you."

Patrick "Rick" Gill's mind immediately latched onto the image of his mother. How was she handling it? It had always been her men who'd been out there facing the danger. Her father, her husband, Rick, and Jimmy in jets. Her agony had always been at home, worrying about one of them. Never before had Mame herself been

166

exposed to . . . to the . . . cutting edge. He wondered how she was bearing up.

"Your folks are okay, far as anyone knows at this point," Clancy continued in his super-cool, laidback way.

"Any casualties at all?"

"Not as far as NASA's telling."

"What are they doing? What's the drill?"

"All I can squeeze out of the folks at Johnson is the fact they got trouble and that they're planning a once-around abort."

Rick looked at his watch.

"Then they should be down now."

"You're right."

"Sounds peculiar."

"We've been alerted, too."

"Why us?" *Titan* was scheduled to land in California, New Mexico backup.

"Just in case. We're on alert to scramble in case of Mexico."

"*Mexico?*"

"Look, Ricky. I just pass on what I hear."

"Okay. Keep me posted."

"Roger."

He put the phone down. There was no point saying more. Bobby wasn't one for small talk, for coloring in the minor details.

Abruptly, the room was filled with all manner of images, notions, voices and faces of his family, a host of memories. All kinds of technical details also crowded into his mind, along with some scare pictures, as well.

Aboard *Titan*. T plus two-hundred-nine minutes.

Taggart's voice came in loud and clear—five by five.

"*Titan*, we have a matter to discuss with you. We suggest you get John Tillinghost up there with you."

"We copy, Houston," Pepper responded. "What is this heavy matter?"

"Location of landing."

"You want Tillinghost in on it?"

"Affirmative, *Titan*."

"Will do."

"We'll wait on the line."

John Tillinghost was fighting down nausea. Inside, he was a mess. It was one thing to design a system, to create something like *Titan*. It had been a monument to him, the ultimate high for his pride. It was something altogether different to ride such a creation to his death. Suddenly, he reflected, it trivializes the whole matter, makes it merely a sophisticated version of the untutored kid strapping on homemade wings and plummeting to his death from a barn roof.

"Mister Tillinghost."

At first he didn't hear.

"Mister Tillinghost?"

It was the Payload Technician—Stewardess, Judy something-or-other. She looked like a damned Indian princess.

"Yes?" he croaked.

"The commander'd appreciate your presence on the flight deck."

Tillinghost was sorely tempted to refuse. He really wanted to deliver a discouraged message to the young woman to pass on to the astronaut in command. "Why don't you let me die in peace?" he'd like to have asked. "Why don't you grinning optimists give me a little time to make my peace with . . . with . . . this desperate situation? Nothing we can say or do can do any good at all. We're all going to burn up!"

But as appropriate as all this might have been to the situation, all those missing tiles, he chose not to deliver it. As strongly as he believed all these things, delivering them in such form, in so many words, would mysteriously have the effect of pushing them toward fulfillment. With an immense sense of weariness and futility, he pushed himself out of the womblike couch and moved obediently after the woman to yet another meeting about what he was becoming more and more convinced was a totally hopeless situation.

"If you head in on this orbit," the voice from Houston explained tersely, "you can make Mexico City. We're ready to help you out there."

"Mexico City?" Pepper asked, rather disgusted. "Why did you pull that one out of the hat?"

"Sombrero," Sager corrected.

"Because it's there, baby. 'Cause it's there!" came the voice of Jim Taggart at Houston Control. "We feel that's the only practical landing site with your present fuel and orbit situation."

"Any special problems?" asked Sager.

"Got to make the mountains, that's all." Taggart came back cheerily.

"We'll watch those pretty damned close," said Sager.

Tillinghost approached. "What's your problem?" he asked warily.

"Our problem," Pepper said. He was all business. "If we're going to get down somewhere reasonably hospitable, we're going to have to burn shortly."

"What's the landing site?"

"Mexico City."

"God," Tillinghost said.

"That bad?"

"Runway's too short, elevation too high for sufficient drag on the landing."

"Don't you think we can make it?"

Tillinghost shook his head. It was hard to summon the spit to speak aloud.

"We have no cross range off the orbital track," Sager put in.

"But Mexico's within that," Pepper said.

"Any other suggestions?" Sager asked.

"Stay up a while, find a better location when we're back over the States."

"Can we stay up that long? Won't take long for the life support gas to run out," Sager put in.

"Not many choices, are there?" Tillinghost asked.

"Not too many," admitted the commander.

"One thing I don't understand," Tillinghost said.

"Yessir?"

"Don't understand that we have a problem from the track we should be on. If the orbital inclination is 38 degrees, the best place I can figure is good old Edwards." The designer held up a mimeographed sheet with orbit track diagrams.

"We're 28.5 degrees," Sager corrected him. "We launched at 90-degree azimuth to rendezvous with *Spacelab*. We have no U.S. real estate under us."

For a moment the designer forgot his sick stomach, his fear of death. One could see the calculations going on inside his head. His eyes were the clue. No matter how emotions may have been chewing at him, if one mentioned numbers to John Tillinghost, he was gone, totally lost to anyone or anything.

170

"Go for it," he said. "I agree. We got to bite the bullet."

On another orbit.

They were frightened, upset, deeply worried about themselves and those they'd left aboard *Titan*. Ian Stafford could appreciate all that. But why did they have to be so bloody difficult to get along with?

Despite the fact that all available space in zero G craft can be crowded like a fishtank, with three dimensions for stowing people instead of gravity's two, they were still painfully crowded. People on bulkheads, overheads, decks, there was precious little room left in the center for people to move through. And swimming through was difficult. The most effective way to get from place to place was to push off. The principal problem with that, however, was the fact that it was difficult to know just how much force to use. There was always a temptation to use too much. As a result, there were many collisions, more than a few bruises from bouncing off walls and cabinets.

Near Houston.

The young woman trembled, turned off the television. The broadcast media were filled with talk of *Titan*. Despite Space Star's official public relations releases and a number of official announcements from NASA's Johnson Space Center, speculation was running wild. Network commentators were positing all sorts of grievous speculations, frightening subtexts for the official pronouncements.

She would listen to no more.

It had been a while since she'd seen her father-in-law,

her mother-in-law. Yet it was easy to visualize them somewhere whirling about the planet. Leon Gill would have his jaw firmly set, his blue eyes alive and electric. Mame Gill would be wide-eyed, taking it all in, courageous, never one to be outdone by any man, especially the one she married.

She wondered about their son, her husband.

How was he bearing up under it? It seemed important to find out.

It had been a while—three months.

Her pretty face reflected concern, then a kind of determination. She reached for the phone.

Before her fingers brushed the black bakelite surface, however, she stopped. She shook her head.

There was still the issue between them. She didn't want to be married to an astronaut. Especially, she didn't want to be married to Astronaut Patrick Gill. There were clearly some men who could handle it—his father, for example.

His father could take the pressure. His father could take the pain. His father could handle the praise; the adulation would roll off him like water from a duck's back. But Rick?

That was an altogether different story. There was still that damned issue!

New York, Los Angeles, Chicago, Atlanta, Portland, Maine. It made little difference where.

Americans clustered around their television sets, kept an ear tuned on their radios. What would the next move be?

There were peculiar things, things no one could yet get a handle on, taking place in *Titan*'s innards in the vicinity of Main Number Three.

Mysteriously, the odor of burning rubber, of ammonia, was beginning to permeate the first-class compartment as well as the airlock. The spacecraft's limited ability to purify and renew the atmosphere was being taxed to the utmost.

"What do you think about the atmosphere back there?" Pepper asked his second-in-command after Judy Langenberg's third communication that things were deteriorating rapidly in terms of breathable air.

They had decided to move as many passengers as possible into the shuttle anyway. Both they and the shuttle designer felt it would be safer for reentry under the circumstances.

"Get 'em on the mid-deck," Sager said. "While we still can."

They'd already discussed the plan as a provisional move. With the women on *Spacelab*, they could just about cram everyone forward.

"Should we wait a bit longer?"

"I wouldn't."

"Why?"

"If we let it get worse, then do it, we risk heavy contamination in here."

"What about heat buildup from all the bodies."

"We can always do a few barbecue rolls."

Sager spoke of a mechanical way to maintain favorable temperature aboard the shuttle. Periodic rotation of the vessel on its centerline axis like a spitted lamb took full advantage of the sun's warming light on one hand, the deep cold of space on the other.

"How many we got back there?"

"Twenty-six."

"God! Where do we put 'em?"

"Sixteen below, the rest up here."

173

"Can we keep a few in the airlock 'til reentry?"

"Possible."

Pepper again looked very haggard, strained. Sager noted it and it worried him.

"Do it," the commander said at last.

Sager punched a button. "Judy," he called. "This is Pete."

"Langenberg here," came the alert, very-much-in-control voice from the first-class compartment.

"Move your people up here."

"Say again?"

"We propose you move your remaining passengers into the flight decks and mid-deck. We feel the atmosphere will be more breathable, safer, and it'll be more secure bringing this baby in."

"Good deal."

"Pick about ten polite ones for riding on the flight deck. The rest can go to mid-deck."

"Ten?"

"That's right. We want to have a cozy little gathering up here."

"Sounds cozy, all right."

He heard what sounded suspiciously like a giggle.

Judy Langenberg certainly had her lid screwed on properly.

One after another, with Fittipaldi's physical urging, with Polikov's golden tongue, with Judy's friendly insistence, the passengers were all pried out of their hiding places. On the flight deck would be Tillinghost, Gill, Waddell, Speaker of the House Claude Meakin, yachtsman Benton Sprigg, Ward, a reporter from Cleveland, the two Saudis, and novelist Polikov. The rest of them, including the Prince of Luxembourg, Locke, and Judy herself, would seek refuge on the spaceship's mid-deck.

Gradually they settled down to make the most of their new spots, strapping themselves in as best they could. It was a quiet group, sober, very much aware of the short span of man's life, his mortality.

12

TITAN was over Africa on her third orbit.

"What's the next move?" Sager asked, keeping his eyes on the thruster indicators.

There was no answer.

"We're going to have to be right on this one," the pilot added, still talking to his spacecraft commander without looking over at him.

There was a sound, half grunt—half wheeze.

"What's the matter? What the hell's the matter?"

Pepper seemed to be sitting with the back of his skull retracted as far as possible between his shoulders. He stared straight ahead, eyes wide open, apparently totally unfocused. His lips were parted and there was saliva at the corner of his full mouth—floating off, bead by gleaming bead.

"Jay, what in God's name is the matter?"

There was no reply.

"Langenberg," Sager called out.

Judy was somewhere below on the mid-deck. Others passed the word.

"What's wrong?" came the question from a drawn-looking John Tillinghost.

"Beats me. Something's got the skipper."

The spacecraft commander was still hunched and immobile, still staring off into space.

Gently, Sager leaned across and shook his arm.

"Jay. Please tell me what's the matter?"

"He is breathing, isn't he?" Tillinghost asked, staring at the astronaut in horror.

There was nothing coherent in Pepper's eyes, no sign, no signal of any kind. There was only a sort of emptiness that seemed to throw itself at the mercy of all present.

"I don't understand what can be the matter with him?" repeated Tillinghost.

Gill approached.

"What's happening?" someone else called out.

"Pepper! Pepper!" Gill was shouting in the astronaut's ear.

Judy Langenberg had managed to find her way through the three-dimensional tangle of bodies to the flight deck.

"He's away," she stated quietly. "Gone for a while."

"Wonder if he'll be back?" asked Sager.

There was nothing sarcastic in the way he said it. It was more a kind of wondering sadness.

"Got to snap him out of it," said Tillinghost, his voice seeming to go up in pitch as he said it. "We . . . we need all the . . . skill we can get."

"I can handle this aircraft," Sager put in drily. "I have all the documentation to prove it."

"But it's a two-man—"

"What about Senator Gill?" asked the Prince of Saudi Arabia.

Gill shook his head. The gesture was emphatic.

"I don't know this spacecraft," he said.

Sager answered the problem quickly, decisively.

177

"We have a qualified pilot aboard." He turned away from the console. "Judy, I want you flying in the right-hand seat."

For an instant, Payload Specialist Langenberg looked startled, just the tiniest bit scared. But her tone was firm and confident when she responded.

"Whatever you say, Pete."

She had wanted to call him skipper, but there was something awkward about using the word in front of Jay Pepper. As out of it as the command pilot seemed to be, there was no way she wanted to strip him of his last bit of dignity, even to bolster Sager.

"That settles it," said Sager.

"Are you sure?" Tillinghost demanded.

"I'm in command until such time as Commander Pepper may tune back and—"

"You'd take that chance?" challenged Tillinghost.

"If I'm convinced he's all right," said Sager.

"*Titan*, this is Houston. We'd like to check out your second—"

"No time to talk," Sager broke in on their message. "No time for discussion," he repeated. "Will call you back."

There was no question whatever that he had assumed command.

"Now let's get a few bodies moved around in here. I want the commander out of the control area and I want Astronaut Langenberg in the seat I currently occupy."

It was a tricky business getting Pepper out of his seat. It wasn't so much his weight, for gravity, all its laws and limitations, had been suspended. It was the crowding of the space, unlike that of earthly space, where everyone stays on the floor. In a spacecraft, real crowding becomes three-dimensional, with people occupying positions on

178

what would normally be considered ceilings, walls. There were even people who hovered in the middle of the available space. As the game of "chairs" proceeded, it had to be made clear to everyone just where he was to move.

Finally, it was done.

Judy occupied the copilot's seat. Pete Sager had moved over into the command position.

"*Titan*, are you ready to give us a status report?" came the voice of Jim Taggart from Houston.

"Affirmative, Houston," said Sager.

"We're listening."

"We have another problem up here, Houston. Commander Pepper has just gone catatonic on us. He's totally out of it."

"*Say again?*"

Even the depersonalizing medium of radio couldn't disguise Taggart's dismay.

"He's . . . withdrawing in some way we don't understand. Won't speak. Won't move. Doesn't seem to focus his eyes properly."

There seemed to be a confused pause on the other end of the connection.

"I've assumed command of the spacecraft," Sager went on, sounding very calm and very sure of himself. "Astronaut Langenberg is in the right-hand seat."

"We copy," the Cap-Com replied. "Stand by for . . . for Flight Director Chandler."

"Standing by."

There was a long pause.

Chandler's hands were shaking slightly—a purely involuntary thing he viewed more with curiosity than dismay. His voice was under good control. "Can you discuss this with one of our psychiatrists, Pete?"

"We can," Sager replied, "but there's not a lot of time."

Chandler nodded his head, forgetting that the man with whom he spoke couldn't see him.

"You got a point there, *Titan*."

"I honestly don't see as there's any time to straighten him out. The important thing's getting this bus back in the garage."

Despite his obvious discomfiture, Chandler found himself smiling. There was something about Sager you could depend on to go to the heart of the matter, to bring the conversation back to earth. He hoped Pete could do as well with *Titan*.

"We agree," Chandler said, trying hard not to append a heavy sigh to the end of his suddenly rendered decision. "Wish your new copilot well," he added.

"Thank you, sir," Langenberg came back herself.

"Houston out," Chandler said, flipping off his microphone.

All shifts were on at Cape Canaveral, Kennedy Space Center. Pad 39B was like a piece of food dropped at a picnic. It was crawling with tiny, purposeful figures.

They worked madly with an incredible sense of urgency, thousands of them, focused on the shuttlecraft *Atlantis*. They had doubled up on normal schedules, volunteered extra hours, extra checks. No one was worried about breaks, lunches even. More than ever the scene evoked resonances of ancient pyramid building, some example of cathedral construction from another time.

"How we doing?" was the question heard most often.

"We're gettin' there," came the answer on the odd

chance that whoever asked was moving slowly enough to hear the reply.

Work progressed at an amazing pace.

"We gonna' blow you away on this one," said Graham McGettigan, the labor leader, to a sweating, shirt-sleeved Oates.

"If we live through it."

McGettigan gave the Space Star executive a look.

"Our living's not the issue, is it?"

Oates grinned. "Not quite," he agreed.

Spacelab.

Boredom was becoming a factor.

They sat there, hovered there, held on to something to keep themselves relatively stable. There was little conversation. They had already expressed concern for the menfolk on the *Titan.* Whatever concern they had for their own situation was, for the most part, held back inside.

Ian Stafford was happy to have them quiet. The less they spoke, the less they moved around, the longer the oxygen would hold out. Further, space was at a premium. *Spacelab* had not been made for guests. As a matter of fact, it had been originally designed as a work platform to be used as an extension of the shuttlecraft orbiter.

"How long's it going to take?" Betsey Garson wailed again.

It was at least the fiftieth time.

"Forever," someone came back wearily.

"Why don't they come?"

"They're waiting for you to die."

Betsey Garson began to curse ardently, seeking to

181

blacken the other woman's character, her name, all her relations. It was a breathtaking recital.

Mame Gill got into it. "Let's remember we're all in this together," she said for the benefit of the others.

Then to Betsy Garson she said: "I belted you once. I can do it again. And I'm very, very willing."

Once again the interior of the crowded space station became silent.

It was a surreal place with forms floating around free, few lights burning. The feeling of fear was still thick in the air.

Mame Gill was close to Stafford.

"How goes it?" she asked. She spoke softly.

"By the book," he said.

"Are we conserving?"

"It's all right."

Actually, it was anything but all right. He was lying, at least evading. It was becoming clear to him that fear—gut fear—makes the human being suck up more oxygen.

He was interrupted, saved from lying further.

The radio began to crackle. "*Spacelab*, this is Houston."

Stafford made his way to the communications console.

"*Spacelab* here," he said.

"We have a piece of hopeful news for you, *Spacelab*. Here are the new coordinates for your rendezvous with *Atlantis*."

"Jolly good, Houston. Do they include an ETA?"

"Sorry about that," responded the Houston voice. "Everything but the time."

"Oh well," said Stafford. "Ready to copy."

Wide-eyed, the refugees, nerves agitated at a variety of pitches, listened to the numbers—none of which they understood or really knew how to interpret. What they understood, however, was the bottom line. Hearing those unintelligible numbers did lend great encouragement that within a reasonably short period of time they'd be rescued.

There was no joy expressed overtly, no cheering or loud laughter. There were a few quiet smiles and one could feel a subtle ebb of tension. A few of the refugees even managed to doze off.

"What about *Titan*?" someone called out in a small, scared voice just as Stafford concluded his conversation with Johnson Space Center.

"Soon," the big Englishman said, looking at the chronometer strapped to his wrist.

"Soon?"

"They'll be reentering soon."

The networks were staying with it. All regular broadcasts had been superseded.

The attracive, very concerned face of a blond woman in her mid-thirties filled the TV monitor. In a voice balancing great self-control with growing concern, she said:

"Spaceship *Titan*, launched approximately three and one-half hours ago from Kennedy Launch Center at Cape Canaveral, continues to experience great but unspecified difficulties. NASA officials admitted moments ago that there have been injuries aboard the spacecraft. They refused to specify either the nature or severity of those injuries, but it was conceded for the first time that there is official concern for the safety of those aboard.

"There is, however, some cause for optimism as the transfer of all women and children to *Spacelab* has been accomplished, apparently without incident, and space officials indicate that the preparation of *Atlantis*, rescue

183

shuttle for those aboard the European Space Agency's spacecraft, is well ahead of schedule."

"My God," said an alarmed bartender in Chicago. "It sounds more like *Titanic* than *Titan!*"

"Women and children?" commented a viewer in Denver, another in San Pedro, and yet others from Madawaska, Maine, to Houston's suburbs. "Sounds more like a sinking than a spaceflight!"

On the crowded flight deck there was a short breathing space in the full schedule.

"What are you doing here anyway?" Sager demanded abruptly.

The way he asked the question gave Judy Langenberg the impression that there was no one else present. It was as if the two of them were altogether alone, tuned out on the rest of the world, despite the cluster of people above them, below them, beside them.

"I've asked myself that."

"And what was the answer?"

"A mixed bag of thoughts."

"How come I never really got to know you?"

She chuckled. "How much time did any of you hotshots have for us latecomers?"

"Score one for your side."

There was a pause.

She began to speak in that same intimate way he'd begun the conversation, ignoring the presence of anyone else.

"I'm the youngest of five girls," she explained. "Four older sisters, big and blond, real Scandinavian women—great figures. Then I came along, little and dark, an ugly duckling."

184

Sager snickered. He saw nothing even remotely ugly about her.

"My father, a pilot, wishing and waiting for a boy, saw the handwriting on the wall. I was just different enough, just ill-favored enough, so I was chosen to be the pilot in the family. I became the son he put in his cockpit seat. I've been flying as long as I can remember."

Sager nodded his head slowly, grinning.

"Damned glad to have you sitting beside me, son," he said.

"Thanks a lot."

He sneaked a look across. "And anybody who calls you an ugly duckling must be out of his damn mind."

"Thanks again, Pete," she said as the head of one of their passengers seemed to float nearby.

Suddenly the mood was broken. Sager was all business.

"Now let me feed you some of these numbers we're gonna' need to get this sad-assed bird home."

"Ready when you are, skipper."

Taggart's voice was still maintaining its matter-of-factness, its cheery self-assurance. Somehow he still managed to sound like an earnest Boy Scout working for his merit badge in amateur radio.

"*Titan*, this is Houston," he said. "we have a go on the Mexico City option."

"*Olé!*" came Sager's slightly raspy baritone.

"Repeat?" Taggart asked.

"*Olé!* As in three cheers or fantastic," Sager explained. "It's nice to know there's somewhere down there to go."

"Thought you'd like that," Taggart added. "And you'll be more than welcome anywhere you can set that ship of yours down."

"What about the runway?" came Sager's voice.

"We've been assured they're ready for you."

"Thank you kindly."

Somehow Taggart, sitting there in front of the great mass of hardware, in the midst of all the technological complexity of Mission Control, found himself all but overwhelmed with the human dimension of what he had become a minor part of. Surely *Titan* was a mechanical contrivance, a vast collection of some of the most complex and marvelous creations of man. But the essence of her, the central reality of the mission, was the human being. Pepper and Sager and Langenberg were out there with a truckload of people—people with families, with problems, with all sorts of ties to the rest of mankind.

You're their lifeline!

The words echoed loud and clear in his conscious mind.

You're their link to the world of men and women! You're their connection with earth!

"*Titan*, what's your status?" he broke in suddenly, rending the silence.

"Clown car at the circus," Sager replied. "It's a mite crowded. Temperature's beginning to get a little warm despite the fact we're not into reentry mode. A little stuffy, but otherwise okay."

There was something very brave about the voice on the other end of the connection. For once, Taggart was unable to take the bravery for granted. For once, he found it getting to him.

"Little personal message, Peter."

"We're all ears."

"Make it, buddy. We're pulling for you."

"We copy that."

That was it—the whole exchange.

186

13

For a time there was silence. There was no traffic on the radio frequency assigned to the spacecraft. There was no conversation aboard *Titan*. There was little to say that hadn't already been said. The Indian Ocean worked and surged on the blue planet below them.

Finally, there came the fat-frying sound of the radio transmitting.

"Stand by, *Titan!*" came Taggart's voice.

"Standing by," Judy acknowledged.

"On my count of twenty, for your reentry burn," said the Cap-Com, still calm, reassuring.

"Roger, Houston. We copy," said Judy from the right-hand seat.

"Twenty . . . nineteen . . . eighteen . . ."

Judy showed a peculiar, strained look on her face. Pete looked over curiously.

"Eleven . . . ten . . . nine . . . eight . . ."

But she was doing splendidly. Sager was damned pleased with her performance in all respects.

"Three . . . two . . . one . . . mark!"

She acted.

"Got it, Houston," she came back coolly.

"Outstanding."

They were coming over Australia—its extreme western end.

The reactivated ground station at Woomera, Australia.

A leathery young man sat at a radio console. His tanned face was crinkled with emotion as he spoke.

"Go for it, Yank!" he encouraged. "This is Woomera wishing you chaps the best!"

"Right nice of you," said Judy Langenberg.

"Say again?" said the startled Aussie.

"This is *Titan*," Judy's husky but obviously female voice replied. "We're much obliged for your good wishes."

"Drop in some time and pop a tinnie with us," said the group controller enthusiastically.

"We'll keep that in mind, Woomera."

As the Aussie completed his transmission, he leaped from his chair as from a catapult. "Can you believe," he shouted, "there's a bird in that damn bird!"

The sunny parlor of a convalescent center where a fragile gray man sat hunched forward, tense, eyes fixed on the screen, arthritic hands like knotted line in his skinny lap.

Two women stood well behind him, in earnest discussion.

"He hasn't moved for nearly four hours," the aide told the nurse.

"Have you been able to get him to eat anything?"

"He won't eat until . . ." she gestured at the television which was again showing a simulation of how the shuttlecraft linked up with *Spacelab*.

"I understand," said the nurse. She sounded almost kindly.

The aide had never felt comfortable with that particular nurse, but she ventured forth nevertheless with what she wanted to say. "I know it's not my business to suggest anything like this, but I . . . I think . . . we ought to just let him set there until things . . . kind of sort themselves out."

She waited for the rebuttal.

The nurse surprised her. "I think you're absolutely right," she said. "Leave Mister Langenberg there until . . . until . . ." She didn't finish. She only shrugged and walked away.

The television picture had the watching millions back at Kennedy in Florida. *Atlantis*, appearing a total replica of *Titan*, stood on Launch Pad 39B.

"We are about to have an announcement from Launch Control here at the Kennedy Space Center," said the network commentator.

A gray-haired man with a fleshy face appeared on camera.

"Due to unprecedented efforts on the part of all concerned, it appears that we have sliced by four or five times the time needed to get the orbiter *Atlantis* launched. Within a matter of hours we expect to launch this spacecraft to take *Titan*'s passengers off *Spacelab*."

"Did you hear that, Mister L?" asked the aide, coming over to where the old man sat staring. "They'll be up there in a few hours to rescue your daughter."

The old man didn't smile. "Shouldn't be," he muttered, shaking his head.

"What?"

The old man looked at her with angry, red-rimmed eyes. "She should be 'board that shuttle where she belongs!"

189

The aide simply didn't understand what he was talking about. She reflected again on the terrors of senility.

On one level, Taggart despised being there in the middle of it. There was nothing he could do to affect the outcome. It tore him up. There was something about being stuck there, powerless, that drove him wild. Yet, even as he struggled with that aspect of his situation, he had misgivings about leaving it.

How, you sad-assed fool, do you think you're going to be able to live without it? How, you dumb creature, do you suppose you'll be able to derive any satisfaction out of anything else? Selling soap, designing weapons, building swimming pools, teaching materialistic little dodos to do this or that in higher education? Could any of those things suffice?

"We'll see you on the other side, Houston," came Sager's distinctive voice. "We're starting to feel that old mother gravity."

"Stay cool," Taggart called out to them.

There was no reply.

Taggart felt Chandler standing over him.

"You got everything crossed?" the big man asked the Cap-Com.

"Everything crossable," Taggart responded, "fingers, toes, the works."

"The Englishman seemed to think they looked all right," Chandler said. He was, of course, whistling in the dark, looking for agreement. If one says something often enough, it's reasonably easy to get the notion it'll happen.

"Said everything looked good except those damned tiles," Taggart responded.

"Everything looked nominal otherwise," the Flight Director insisted.

"That's right, Lou."

Then the big man shook his head. "I'm still not crazy about the angle they're going to have to describe on the landing. Flight path seems a bit short for Mexico City."

"Computers seem to like it."

Chandler said nothing more about it. He simply stood there with a peculiar pained look on his face. Taggart had never seen him look quite like that before. He'd seen him tired. He'd seen him upset. He'd seen him fighting off the flu. He'd never seen him look so frazzled, so licked. It was as if some substantial amount of the tremendous vitality that characterized him had leaked out somehow. His face seemed to have lost much of its definition. His whole being seemed to sag, lacking tone.

"Chief?" Taggart called back over his shoulder.

"Yeah."

"Something I'd like to tell you—even now while the fat's on the fire."

"Shoot," Chandler said. "Guess I can handle damn near anything."

"I'm staying in."

"What?"

"I'm staying in this weird outfit. I'm gonna' stick it out."

"You are?" Chandler began to grin. It wasn't the usual Chandler smile. There was too much on his mind, too much pressing and troubling him. But there was no question that he was pleased.

"I figure that sooner or later you'll get around to me, to the rest of my class. We may be tripping over our gray beards, but we'll get our turn."

"What . . . what turned you around?" Chandler asked.

Taggart hesitated for a moment. It wasn't the kind of thing he found it easy to explain, to put a handle on. But he would try. For Lou Chandler, it was the least he could do.

Gesturing upward with his chin, he said, "It's the guys up there . . . all of them. I know they been giving us a hard time, telling us to cram sand, but there's something about the guts they're showing, the trail they're trying to blaze, that gets to me. Maybe it's kid stuff, but if it is, then I don't give a damn about growing up."

"What if . . . ?" The Flight Director didn't finish, but Taggart knew perfectly well what he meant. There were certain things one simply didn't acknowledge at a time like that.

"No matter what, Lou. I'm in for the duration. If, like you say, we're packing up to leave this damned old place, I don't want anyone saying I was unwilling to lug my share of the baggage."

For a moment at least, Chandler's smile gave some hint of the real, everyday Lou Chandler.

"Thanks, Jimmy," he said. "Thanks a hell of a lot."

After a two-minute burn of the Orbital Maneuvering System engines to slow the shuttlecraft from its speed of 15,200 nautical miles per hour, the decelerating space vehicle, which has been moving upside down and backward in earth terms, flips over and pancakes into the atmosphere tilted upward at about forty degrees.

It's during this stage of the flight, when friction between molecules of air and the skin of the spacecraft meet, that incredible heats are generated. There are points on the shuttle's skin that reach temperatures in excess of 2500° Fahrenheit. About three-quarters of the orbiter's external surface is swathed in the silica fiber tiles that give it its mock designation, "flying brickyard." It's also during this portion of the flight that ground communications, the delicate contact between orbiter crew and land stations, are blotted out by the incredible heat of entry.

The BOQ room at Ellington Air Force Base seemed downright unfriendly—not merely neutral. It seemed to glare at him with heavy hostility as he hurried inside to pick up his gear. He left the door open behind him.

Maybe the walls and the window were showing resentment for the fact he'd all but abandoned them lately as the loneliness began to get to him.

Quickly, he scooped up the things he'd come for—clean socks, jockey shorts, shirts, toothbrush.

The phone rang.

"Not home," he muttered.

There was a strong temptation to let the damned thing ring unheeded. No one had to know he was in the neighborhood. He was under orders to get to Mexico. With his folks on *Titan*, there was no one else whose call demanded an answer. Almost no one.

Ready to growl, he snatched the receiver from its cradle.

"Gill here," he snarled.

"Rick?"

He hesitated. With difficulty, he swallowed. "Sally?"

"I'm terribly sorry, Rick."

"They're going to be all right," he said. "I . . . I feel it in my bones."

"I'm sorry about . . . everything, Rick. *Everything*."

There was a truly long pause. So many things were

going on inside his head. Was it pity that prompted her to call? Was it a damned false alarm? Could it be that she was taking this particular moment to give him the final boot down the old greased skid-slide? How had either of them ever let it come to this? Was she just twisting his tail?

"I carry my own load of that crap," he said, not altogether sure what he was saying, assenting to, even as he strung the words together. "Things to be sorry for . . . that's what I mean. There's . . . a whole world of things I've got to be sorry for."

"Marrying me?"

"No way!"

"Are you hurting, Rick? Really hurting?"

Was this to set him up? Was she trying to push the knife in a little deeper?

But no. He would answer without . . . without . . .

"Are you?" he countered, still not sure where she was going.

"Sometimes," she admitted. Sally had never been one for readily opening doors on her inner, emotional life, even for him.

"How?" he pressed her.

It took her a second or two to answer. "Yeah," she said at last.

"I hurt, too," he ventured. "Some of it's what's happening with *Titan*."

"What about the rest of it?" She was good at following one question hard on the heels of whatever else came before. There had always been a hell-for-leather relentlessness in Sally O'Brien.

"What's going on in me . . . or better," he replied, "what's *not* going on in me . . . without you."

It came out so damned awkwardly.

194

Rick Gill had never thought of himself as eloquent. Words came to him with considerable difficulty. He was one for doing, rather than commenting or describing. At this point, however, he sought words feverishly, leaping at them, hoping wildly he could select and seize the right one, use it properly, effectively. Somehow he felt that words, *these* words, on *this* occasion, constituted the only effective line he had on Sally. And there was no way in the world he'd let himself relinquish hold of Sally. He couldn't allow her to shake off the last hook, to snap the lead. Maybe it was merely the moment, what was happening to his parents, that had prompted her to call. She *had* called, however. She was on the other end of the line. Suddenly, his life had fallen into focus again.

"Please forgive me, Sal. *Please*. We've got to . . . to put it . . . together again."

He flinched, even as he launched the earnest plea. It was so trite, corny, ordinary. She had every opportunity to come ripping back with some devastating put-down having to do with the vulnerability of the moment. If she wanted to she could kick his ass around the block.

But why had she called in the first place? Why had she?

"I wanted you to say that, Rick. I needed you to say that. I'm with you already, even now before you can get over here and before I can get the bed turned down. It's my place to be with you. We've got to . . . to put all this behind us."

A great weight suddenly dropped off Rick Gill's shoulders. His parents were still in jeopardy. He still hurt inside. There was still unresolved differences between them. It would be hours—days, perhaps—before he could take advantage of that felicitously turned-down bed. But the miracle—the first one at least—had been delivered. He could fly again.

14

The glow outside was gone.

The intense heat was beginning to dissipate. The spacecraft seemed to be intact. They were sweating, uneasy, uncomfortable, but, for the moment, alive.

For the most part, fear had been a stranger to Judy Langenberg. Only now and then had she made his acquaintance, but they'd never actually been introduced. In all her experience as a pilot, in the intense period of her astronaut training, she could vividly recall no feeling of panic, little out-and-out nervousness of any kind.

It hadn't been a matter of having outstanding courage, of mastering some special trick for keeping terror at bay. It had been more a matter of not really being aware of it in the first place. It had been her ability to focus altogether on what she was doing to the exclusion of all else. Judy was one who could concentrate, blot out the nonessential. Many times when she might have been absolved for being scared, she was simply too busy working at something more important, too occupied with the chore at hand to speculate on some conjectural devastation.

This time, however, everything was different.

Judy could feel it. She was sweating even more profusely than the temperature justified. She was finding it difficult to keep her mind on her proper chores. There was a persistent tic in her cheek. It had never happened before.

As *Titan* came hurtling down into the thickening atmosphere envelope of earth, still glowing cherry red from the incredible temperatures of reentry, Judy found herself racked with fear. For some inexplicable reason, the prospect of dying seemed more grievous than it ever had before, more worth worrying about. For the first time she could ever recall, she was vulnerable, honestly so, to the kind of apprehension hitherto experienced only by others.

It was a blow to her self-confidence—her pride.

For a second or so she worried that Pete Sager, right there next to her, might have detected some of that fear. But if her fellow pilot was aware of her discomfiture, he gave no sign. Judy was deeply grateful.

Kenny Jackson had been part of the first flight scrambled to fly *Titan* into New Mexico. They'd been diverted south when it appeared that Mexico City was a possibility.

If *Titan* didn't make it, he wondered, what would there be to see? Would there be some shower of ashes, of incinerated pieces? Or would everything stay outside? Or would there be a melted—

His eyes narrowed.

"Got 'em!" he shouted. "Got 'em!"

Way high and ahead he could make out a tiny speck coming down at an incredible rate of speed.

"Damn thing's flying!" he yelled out, forgetting protocol altogether. "They came through!"

*   *   *

197

There was little holding back in Houston. The hairiest part had been accomplished. *Titan* had not burnt up on her return to the atmosphere. She was still flying. Although there was no way at that particular point to tell how well she was flying, how well situated she was to make it the rest of the way in, one major obstacle had been hurled.

"Go, baby, go!" Lou Chandler shouted, smacking his fist into his large, meaty palm.

The heat was terrific aboard the spacecraft, almost too much to endure. The smell was considerably worse. The flight deck and mid-deck of the shuttle were not made to accommodate such a crowd. The heat of reentry, the close proximity of so much flesh, the over-loading of the shuttle's air-conditioning system were all rendered even more uncomfortable by the fear experienced by people not trained to know what to expect. It was as if panic were beginning to rise up all around them like a ground fog, like smoke.

The two pilots, however, still retained control.

"Eyeball those!" ordered Sager, pointing to a startling vista of mountain peaks along the glide path toward Mexico City.

"Mexico?" Judy Langenberg came back quickly.

"Not the tour book," he insisted roughly. "Relative altitude!"

"We can't make them," she said flatly. "No way we make it over them."

"You win a cigar!"

"And a sendoff," she said. She was talking about an astronaut's funeral. "Cactus blossoms."

"Get us an alternate strip."

"Houston," she transmitted immediately. "This is *Titan*. Need a backup landing field, *muy pronto!*"

"This is Houston. We copy and agree you can't make the mountains. Over."

"Glad you agree. Give us an alternate. Fast!"

There was a brief pause.

"Roger. Take Guadalajara. That's a hard right, *Titan*."

"Be quick with the course," cracked Sager, "or it'll be a hard, *hard* right."

"Heading?" called Judy.

"Try ninety-three degrees from your present heading. That's niner-three."

"*Try* it?" Sager marveled. "What if we don't like it? They gonna' give us another one to play with?"

"Affirmative, Houston. We copy nine-three," answered Judy. "We'll try it!"

"Guadalajara was just under us," Judy said. "I see it to the right. We're not even close to Mexico City."

"We copy," said Houston. "We're bringing you in."

"Gee, thanks," Sager said. "Did you arrange for this or was it the gods?"

"Both. Hard right again, sixty-eight degrees on a new heading of 2–7–1. Eyeball airport, minimize lift vector."

"Roger," she said. "I have the airport sighted."

"Dropping like a rock but still aerodynamic," Sager added. "I have it, Houston."

Somehow Pete Sager was incredibly loose. There was something about the man, Judy noticed, that seemed to flourish under impossible circumstances—like those they were undergoing. It hadn't been the same with poor Jay. He'd been a psychologist's nightmare. They'd stashed him in the stand-up sleep station on the mid-deck. He'd simply frozen like a human Eskimo bar.

199

Pete, on the other hand, seemed to get wilder, noisier, a little more overtly insane than usual, even while his hands, his judgment, remained icy cool, impeccable. Judy had known pilots like Pete before. She was glad to be with one of them right now.

"This damn landing we're about to try is likely going to jar you right outa' your jockey shorts, gentlemen," Pete announced in a loud voice. "Sorry, Judy. Therefore, I want everybody strapped down that's got a strap of some kind to secure himself. For the rest of you, assume a position protecting whatever goodies you've got to guard."

Someone was praying out loud on the mid-deck.

Someone else told him to keep it down.

"Where we goin' in?" asked Gill from behind copilot Langenberg.

Sager answered. "Guadalajara."

"Short?"

"Damned short, I'll bet."

"What's beyond the runway?"

"We'll find out, won't we?"

"No second tries, huh?"

"You got it," Sager said. "This here's a very heavy glider, Senator."

"Can the 'Senator.' There's no damn senate up—"

"You're on the mark," Astronaut Langenberg interrupted. "Hold steady."

"Gotcha'!" Sager responded.

"We gonna' make it?" called Tillinghost.

"Shut up, John!" snapped Gill.

"Thanks," Judy acknowledged.

"Anytime, Astronaut," he said.

It meant a lot coming from him.

* * *

"This is Yellow Leader," called a voice through the radio monitors at Houston Control. "We have visual contact with the spacecraft. Goin' like a bat. Looks intact!"

"How's he look for Guadalajara?"

"Lined up pretty good. Wingman?"

"Maybe four- or five-degree correction required," came another laconic voice.

Taggart picked it up quickly. "*Titan*, you're visual from Air Force units," he said. "Indicate correction required."

"They're maybe four degrees to port," came the voice of one of the fighter pilots.

"Correct to starboard, *Titan*."

"We copy that, Houston. We can handle the required correction," came Langenberg's voice calmly. "We've got a visual fix on their runway." She sounded totally in control of herself.

Chandler sat there at his station, a strange meditative figure. He had the image of Judy's face in his mind. There was something about that mocking, mischievous grin of hers that had always made him furious. Like when his own daughter Chrissie used to toss back "Yessir Cap'n" at him when he'd scold her as a kid. It was non-explosive sedition—foot-dragging, subtle resistance. No matter how hard Training Director Chandler had sought to ride Astronaut-in-Training Langenberg, no matter what detail he'd throw her way, he'd always end up getting that sassy grin.

"Grin, baby!" he muttered under his breath. "Grin!" He meant it. "Keep it all together, babe. Hold on!" He'd have given six months pay to see that same grin back in Houston at that very moment.

"How do they look?" he demanded.

"Far as we can tell, they're on the money," the answer came through.

"Moving pretty fast," came another moderating report. "They gotta' slow it down. Not enough runway for too much heat."

"*Titan*," Taggart broke in alertly. "Your airspeed seems high."

"We copy," came Judy's cool voice. "We'll do what we can."

The space shuttle lands hard.

Twenty times faster than a commercial jetliner, the orbiter descends at fifteen thousand feet per minute. There is little braking power.

It was happening.

It was no dream. They were back on earth, hurtling toward a runway at over 190 knots. It was not a scary story or the result of imagination. The shuttle was touching down. The earth was coming up to meet them.

Time had slowed down. It was as though each second had expanded to a minute, each minute to an hour. Everything was like a slow-motion picture, appearing languorous, graceful, weirdly unhurried.

Judy caught a glimpse of Pete. His face was serious, concentrated, fighting to the very last second to find a solution to the terrible predicament. They were landing too fast. She loved him for his intensity, his stubborn fixation on the problem. There was nothing in the world that so touched her as the dedicated concentration she'd seen in her father, her first flying teachers. Such was, for her, the true measure of manhood.

Somehow they managed to stay upright, in some semblance of control, for the length of the runway, and then, running out of paved surface, the shuttle spun sideways like a Frisbee thrown inexpertly. They were spinning, sliding out of control.

The young prince didn't scream as he saw his father's head break like a fragile egg. He gagged and a portion of him died inside as he tore loose from his safety belt and slammed hard into his parent's lifeless body. But he would utter no desperate sound, no manifestation of grief. He owed it to his father, to their house.

He had no time to utter real prayer. He had time only to utter, "Allah!" before he lapsed into unconsciousness.

Death seemed to be everywhere on the arid Mexican field. There was nothing private about it. Unlike the dominant contemporary manner of leaving the so-called civilized world, tucking final agony behind glass and tile, noncommittal faces, plastic tubing, discreet surgical green, here death was on public display, vulgar, obscene, under the kleig light of brilliant Mexican sunshine.

Broken corpses tumbled from the shattered space shuttle. Two men, apparently injured, yet briefly able to move, scuttled free of the broken spacecraft like insects fleeing before some anonymous exterminator, only to fall dead after inhaling fumes from the violated fuel tanks.

The scene was dominated by chemical odors, popping sounds, clouds of dense brown smoke, white steam.

The centerpiece of this convocation of catastrophe, her Star Space insignia still visible, was *Titan* herself— poor shattered *Titan*.

"*Dios*, look at her!" said the visibly moved airport superintendent. "It is so sad!"

Tears welled from his eyes. His fingers, trembling,

203

touched the flesh of his own throat experimentally as if assuring himself his head was still attached.

"That is the worst of it," he added in a thick voice.

Some maybe wouldn't have approved of his sadness for a mere machine. Some might have been quick to criticize him and the others standing by the scene of devastation and bloodshed, saying, "Save your tears for humans. Why are you wasting your grief on . . . a pile of metal and plastic?"

For those who could share any part of the dream, those who could recognize and cherish the beauty that had existed in her, the sweet curving purity of her lines—for those who could view *Titan* and others like her as the culmination, the fulfillment, of years and centuries of man applying divinely bestowed intelligence to seemingly insoluble problems—the death of *Titan* eclipsed even the individual tragedies of those who perished in her belly.

There was activity across the field.

"Look!" shouted the superintendent. "*Madre!* They're waving!"

Several of the rescue crew, going in with the heavy resignation crews learn to adopt when approaching aeronautical holocaust, waved from the wreck.

Something about their wild semaphore encouraged the grieving, horrified officials and spectators to hope for survivors.

Someone was alive!

The airport manager, along with his security chief, pounded toward the place, feet stumbling, raising dust. No longer constrained by horror to back up their own prudence, both men, followed by several aides, galloped like giraffes toward the stricken spacecraft.

"How many?" they began shouting madly, even before they were close enough to make themselves heard.

"Cuantos tiene usted?"

"What condition?"

It would be moments before any answers would be available, but there was joy, nonetheless, a sudden, almost blinding surge of hope.

15

A CLOSEUP of a news commentator's face—unsmiling. It made little difference which network, which individual newsreader. The message was the same.

"NASA has just announced that the shuttlecraft *Titan* has touched down in Guadalajara, Mexico. The orbiter has apparently crashed upon landing. There are unconfirmed reports coming out of Mexico that some have survived.

"At the moment, we have no numbers and no names. Details are scantily available at this time. We will, however, keep you informed!"

Judy was surprised but grateful when she opened her eyes. Clearly, she was alive. There was some pain, some discomfort. Her left leg felt numb. There was an active throbbing in her wrist. She had to force herself to focus in order to know it was her left wrist. She tried to lift her head to look at it, but discovered she was too weak, too drained by . . . whatever it was that had happened.

"Woman," came a husky male voice. "You . . . you still . . . with us?"

She remembered Pete Sager. It was his voice from somewhere close by, somewhere behind her.

"Think so," she answered.

"You hurt?"

"Somewhere, but it's not . . . not too bad, I think."

Sirens sounded somewhere nearby. They were unusual sirens, especially strident.

"They're talking Spanish," Sager said.

"What?"

"Even the damn sirens."

Judy discovered the hard way that it really hurt to laugh.

"You okay, Pete?"

"If I could get half of my body to work right."

"Won't ask which half."

"Better not."

They made no special effort to move. Actually, it would have proven difficult, for part of the control console was pushed back, pinning them securely in place. There was also the danger of venting gases, of explosions. It would be far better to lie still, wait for rescue.

"What about the rest of them?" Judy wondered aloud. "Our passengers."

"*We're* alive."

It disappointed her to hear him speak so. She wanted, for some reason, to have him show a lively concern for his passengers, *their* passengers. It was part of the tradition in which she'd been whelped as a commercial pilot before undergoing astronaut training.

"They say the pilot's first one at the crash site," he observed. "If he makes it . . . there's . . . there's a pretty good chance everyone else can . . . make it, too."

That was considerably better.

"You sound all right," she observed.

"I'd like to be able to show you."

"Huh?"

"You're one hell of a piece of work, lady."

The silence that followed hard upon that particular statement felt good—damned good. It was a compliment to her flying ability and, it seemed, just a bit more than that. Whatever he meant by it, it surely did give her a glow.

"If we make it out of here . . . how about . . ." he began.

"How about what?"

There was yet another pause.

"I'm lying in a . . . a kind of . . . funny position to be . . . propositioning my copilot."

"Well," she responded impulsively, "I'm lying in a damned strange position to say yes."

The network commentator broke into the general coverage of the *Titan* mission with further news from Mexico.

"Rescue personnel at Guadalajara report that at least nine people have survived the crash landing of the space orbiter *Titan*. Late reports indicate that two of the spacecraft's pilots are among the survivors, including the woman astronaut who was one of those actually piloting the shuttle when it reentered earth's atmosphere. Within moments we expect to have pictures taken at the scene by Mexican television personnel."

The old man grinned.

"She did it!" he shouted.

The nurse's aide was standing just behind him.

"I'm so happy for you, Mister Langenberg!" she said, all but squealing in her enthusiasm. It appeared that his daughter had somehow survived the terrible crash they'd just witnessed on some grainy footage borrowed from Mexican TV.

"She did the big deed!" he shouted enthusiastically. "Damn if she didn't!"

For the first time in weeks he was on his feet, moving around the room, grinning mightily.

"Knew she'd do it," he said, again and again. "Knew it all along."

"That's wonderful, Mister Langenberg," called the shift nurse, hurrying into the patients' day room. She had apparently discovered the news somewhere else. "We're all very happy for you and your daughter."

"She flew the damned thing!" crowed the old man. "She did it! I knew she could!"

The nation was stunned.

Americans were not ready to lose on this particular front. Though there was an element of heroism in the *Titan* flight, and some relief that there had been survivors, that all had not died, there was an element of shock in having lost the spacecraft. The day passed by quickly. The networks stalled for time, awaiting fresh news out of Mexico.

It was slow coming, NASA and the Mexican government being reluctant to release details until they were ready.

The man being moved to the hospital plane for transfer to the United States clasped the battered notebook, cradling it like a baby or some favored pet against his chest.

"What you got there?" asked an Air Force nurse assigned to assist in the transfer.

"Notes on what happened."

"You mean . . . you wrote down what was going on?"

"Everything I could," answered novelist Polikov. "Every damn thing I could jot down, got scribbled."

"That's . . . weird," she observed.

"Yeah," he smiled as his litter was passed up onto the lift. "It certainly is. Why would anyone want to hear about . . . us?"

There was frightful tension in a modest brick house in Springfield, Delaware County, Pennsylvania. A Pennsylvania State Police car was parked in front of the house, a TV Action News van across the street.

It was late, or early, depending on how one chose to look at it.

There'd still been no direct word from Mexico, no word from Space Star or the government. Everyone was still in the dark. The Fittipaldi children sat dumbly by the telephone. They looked dazed. Most of the reporters had been pulled back into a sort of holding pattern, and the phone company had placed an intercept on the telephone to keep the line clear for official callers. Previously they'd had calls from exploiters, reporters from everywhere, cranks, and well-wishers.

"There's no way," nineteen-year-old Mark kept repeating over and over, from his seat in the corner of the room. "There's no way they can be lost."

"Shut up," seventeen-year-old Jerry kept telling him.

"There's no way my old man can be dead."

"We know Ma's all right," said Penny.

"We don't actually know that," said Paul. "They gotta' get her back, don't they?"

"They're gonna' launch first thing in the morning."

They were on edge, all of them, as far as any sort of assertions were concerned.

"Why did he go?" Penny asked.

210

"What the hell does *that* mean?" Paul challenged. He seemed closest to the breaking point.

"I mean it was crazy."

"He's never done it," Jerry said with a funny grin. "He's never done it before, never been there before. He got a chance to do it, so he did it. Don't you even understand your own father?"

She shook her head.

"I . . . I guess I don't."

"Don't you know that's the way he works? Don't you know that's what's rumbling around inside him all the time? There's something crazy about him. There's something about the man that simply doesn't work the way things work in other people. He's perfectly capable of doing something for the sheer hell of it."

"Yeah," Mark suddenly piped up. "Remember the time he took off for the hockey game in Montreal?" Mark had been only eleven.

"What?" Penny asked. "I don't remember that."

"You were just a kid at the time."

She snickered. Penny was the oldest of the Fittipaldi kids.

"He drove all day to get to the damned hockey game, then all night to get home," Jerry added, chuckling.

But Penny wasn't to be put off with recollections about hockey games or some of the exotic sports her father followed with enthusiasm.

"Why'd he do this, though? Why?" Penny's brown eyes were filled with tears. They used to say she had her father's eyes. It used to make her angry. Now she wasn't so sure.

There were tears in Jerry's eyes. But there was pride in his voice—a lot of pride—as he said, "Because he's

211

Pop. And you know and you, and you, and I, that we'd feel like shit if he was any other way!"

It sank in. For several minutes they all sat there silently.

"Let's pray," Penny said finally, eyes suddenly dropping.

"What the hell you think we've been doing if we haven't been praying?" snorted Paul.

Then weakly, but honestly, the Fittipaldis laughed. It felt good.

They lightly sedated Mary Fisher just in case.

She had taken it well, bravely, like the tough, gutsy woman Ron would have wanted her to be. But it hurt. Damn, but it hurt.

She wanted to thank the crew—the astronauts who had treated Ron so well, made room for him. She wanted to thank them for . . . for bringing him home the only way they were able to.

"How are they?" she asked Chandler. She had somehow gotten through to him on the telephone. Even doped up, she managed to use the telephone.

"Miz Fisher, I'm damned sorry," he kept saying. "You don't know how sorry we all are."

"I know you are, Mister Chandler. But . . . but how are the rest of them, the crew?"

Normally, he wouldn't have told her, but somehow she had the right to know. The calls were still not being made for some reason he'd never understand.

"Pepper's dead, Miz Fisher."

"I'm sorry to hear it."

"Sager and Langenberg made it."

"How are they?"

"Mostly superficial. She's got a broken arm. He's got a concussion."

"Tell them thank you."

"It was Pete who was responsible for bringing him back."

"I owe him."

"We all do."

Oates had Dye on the phone.

"Tell the President we're ready to go at dawn."

"Dawn?"

"Close to it."

"Sure you aren't rushing it?"

Oates face began to swell. He could feel it.

"Rushing it?" he blustered angrily. "Of course we're rushing it. We're rushing it because we've got lives to save. What the hell did you think we're going to do?"

"You're way ahead of schedule," said the Space Adviser to the White House.

"Sometimes we win," said Oates. "And sometimes we lose. On this one—on this part of the whole operation— we're about to win one."

Then, not allowing the man in Washington a word, he hung up the phone.

Ulanov was damned disgusted.

He had wanted to change into a better uniform, shave again before speaking with the big man, but they'd insisted there was no time.

"Hurry up! Hurry up!" the man sent to fetch him had nagged.

Now here he was cooling his heels in an outer office staring at Monius's fat-titted secretary typing some of the

213

mountains of paperwork that he seriously believed would destroy the Soviet space program one day if allowed to go on unchecked.

"He couldn't have wanted to see me very much," he kept saying to the girl.

She would just look up and shrug. It was fun seeing what the shrugging did to her breasts.

Finally, however, the summons came. He was beckoned into the big man's office. He stood there like a young cadet while his superior fiddled with papers, tried to act even more important than he was.

Anyone can play that game, Ulanov told himself. He merely stood there like a stone statue, waiting to see what was on the official's mind. Or was that a contradiction in terms—*mind* and *official*?

"Well, Ulanov?" the man finally said.

What sort of conversational opening was that?

"Well what, sir?"

"Those men were not your friends, Ulanov," the big man said.

"What men are those?" the cosmonaut asked.

"They are not, I repeat, your friends."

"And I repeat, sir," Ulanov came back. "I don't have any idea who you're talking about."

"The Americans."

"Oh." He decided to play it cautious. "I . . . I think I understand . . . what you're . . . saying."

"You damned well better understand."

"I do."

But Ulanov was lying. Inside, he was whistling a totally different tune. Inside, he was saying, "Perhaps not friends, but brothers."

"They crashed," the big man said.

"What?"

214

"They crashed in Mexico."

"Any . . . survivors?"

The big man shrugged. "I don't know."

"You should know," Ulanov said.

The official's eyes narrowed. He sensed the rebellion inside the cosmonaut.

There was rebellion in the man, even as he stood there uncomfortably before the desk of his superior. He hoped that some of his counterparts had escaped the crash. For they were his friends. Those on *Titan* meant far more to him and to his comrades in the company of cosmonauts than anyone in Moscow could ever realize. They were fellow citizens of a higher country, a country he was beginning to believe was the country of the future, the country to which he owed his highest allegiance.

That country was space.

"I want you to retract the foolish statement you all signed."

"I . . . I . . . can't do that, comrade."

"And why not?"

"There are other signatures besides mine."

The man on the other side of the desk smiled nastily, showing his gold teeth. "We have to start somewhere."

Ulanov realized that the disputed statement meant nothing now. It was too late to help *Titan*. Eventually the truth would come out, their allegiance to that higher country would come out clear. Until then, a man had to live.

"What need I do?"

"Sign this," said the big man.

Ulanov did what he was told.

16

Early morning, Washington, D.C.

Though *Titan* had died, the city seemed as usual. Traffic moved. People chatted and laughed. Dogs barked and aircraft moved over on their way to National Airport just across the Potomac.

The congressional delegation strode into the White House like a group of children with mud on their boots. They seemed almost guilty about it. Even though they filed in with a grimness and intenseness of purpose that seemed to suggest they were well within their rights in coming, there was a sort of guilt showing, an attitude that implied all was not a hundred percent well in the whole business.

They were an informal committee, a group that space proponents and supporters in the House referred to as "the foot draggers," "the screaming mimis" or worse.

"The President is expecting you, gentlemen," announced the White House Appointment Secretary. They had phoned ahead to be sure the Chief Executive would see them. "Would you go right into the Oval Office?"

The President stood behind the massive desk as they

were ushered in, his great bulk even more formidable with the broad window behind it. The room smelled of lemon-scented furniture polish and cigar smoke. The TV monitors on which he'd been watching the *Titan* coverage had been moved out of sight.

"Come in, gentlemen," he called out to them.

There were eight who'd come along. It was a bipartisan group. Along with Senator Orton Fletcher of South Dakota were seven Representatives. There was apple-cheeked young Herman Chocotte from Wisconsin, Bill Abernathy from Maryland, and Michael Beston from California. Louis Lerando of Louisiana was much in evidence with his great shock of blue-white hair, as was the dour, bald-headed Anselmo Oriani from Rhode Island. Along also, but looking less than enthusiastic, were Maurice Brattigan of Massachusetts and Len Kidder of Colorado. Bob Menster of Illinois and Carlos Benitez of Arizona were missing, but one had to believe they tagged along in spirit, having so vociferously opposed space programs in the past.

"What are there, eight of you?" demanded the President as they arranged themselves in a semicircle around his desk.

"Along with a hell of a lot of votes from every part of the nation," said Lerando with his characteristic oratorical excess.

"Eight's always an awkward number in politics," quipped the President, choosing to ignore Lerando's remark. He'd heard these brags and threats about votes damn near every time he'd spoken with a legislator. Who'd they think elected him? "Maybe we ought to have the Vice President here in case a tie develops among you."

217

"There's not likely to be a tie here, Mister President," insisted Senator Fletcher. "We agree on this matter."

The degree of enthusiasm seemed to vary somewhat more than Fletcher would have liked. A couple of the Representatives were looking altogether hang-dog.

"Gentlemen, speak your piece!" the President told them.

"Well, first of all, we wanted to assure you that whatever we have to say is most assuredly in the best tradi—"

"Let's say what has to be said," the President broke in.

Fletcher, his face darkening as blood rose to it, was spokesman and he took over.

"Well, I'm sure you're aware, Mister President, as everyone in the world is today, of what's gone on and is still going on up in space. It's a sad and sickening spectacle. Like everyone else, you're perfectly conscious, we're sure, of the fact that we're being sorely humiliated in the eyes of men and nations. This should prove to you and to the people who've supported this program, that the whole thing is wrongheaded and—"

"Bullshit!" interrupted the President of the United States, coloring. "That's unadulterated bullshit and you know it, Orton. It's damned shortsighted idiots like you that make this whole job like pullin' teeth!"

The President allowed his visitors no time to recover from his strong assault.

"When the *Titanic* went to the bottom of the North Atlantic, did that disprove the usefulness of the ocean-going passenger vessel? Or did it tell us that we had to steer a little more carefully and build and handle our ships a little more wisely? Did the fact that we lost a whole regiment of aviators in the formative years of avia-

218

tion mean that the Wrights and Glen Curtis and all the other early pioneers should have stuck with the bicycle?

No one said a word.

"What's been up in the sky all those years since? Is that Pegasus, the winged horse, up there? It seems to me," he lurched angrily onward, "that there's always a bunch of horses' backsides standing around wringing their hands when anything like this happens. I think it would be a practical, damned commendable measure if you'd wring your own necks instead. I can tell you with no reservations, *I'd* rather!"

It was probable that one of the highly affronted Congressmen at that point might have launched into some sort of spirited defense of himself and his colleagues or for the point of view they espoused had they been given time. And it's equally probable that a deeply angry President would have done his best to slap them down again had not an abrupt intervention taken place at that very moment.

A door flew open.

Will Dye, brushing past a startled appointment secretary, moved into the room. He was excited.

"Mister President," he broke in. "*Atlantis* is to be launched in less than five minutes from the Cape. They've clipped off over twenty hours from their best estimate!"

"Somebody wheel that TV monitor back in here!" ordered the man behind the desk, a triumphant smile suffusing his heavy, rather sallow features. "I want to see this launch. I want the satisfaction." Then he looked around belligerently at the group of legislators who were first stunned, then even more uncomfortable. "And I want you, gentlemen, you Cassandras, to stand here

219

with me and watch it fly. I want to hear and see the way you twist and wriggle to keep from believing that we've got the same old American spirit we've always had and that somehow—and I *do* believe it—we'll come through this experience stronger, smarter, more determined than ever before!"

The old boy was really pouring it on. And as Bill Dye listened to him, he again became aware that in this President, NASA, and all those who saw space as important, critical even, to the future of the world, had a true friend.

"Thank you, Mister President," Dye said.

"Thank you?" asked the Chief Executive. "What the hell for?"

"Just, thank you, sir."

The President knew exactly what Dye meant. He grinned and winked back at the man.

It was different this time.

There were no flag-draped grandstands opened up, no military bands, no phalanxes of earthbound spectators invited onto the post. This was strictly a working launch.

But there was something special about it. There was enthusiasm and dedication. There was deep feeling among launch personnel that it was important, critical even, to do everything possible to save a group of their fellow human beings.

There were some press types around. There was no lack of news value in the launch. The networks were covering it. This time, however, there was something gritty, down-to-earth about the coverage itself—no glitz, little glamor.

The countdown went without a hitch.

"Why is it we do better when we're rushed?" asked

one of the engineers watching in the blockhouse of launch control out near the tip of the cape itself.

"Isn't that the way it is in the good old U.S.A.?" commented another NASA technician.

"Thirty seconds and counting!"

"Twenty-nine."

"Twenty-eight."

"Twenty-seven."

An exhausted Tim Oates stood next to an equally spent Graham McGettigan.

"Know any good prayers?" demanded the Space Star executive of the labor leader.

"Remember 'em all."

"Get busy."

The voice on the intercom proceeded:

"Fifteen."

"Fourteen."

"Thirteen."

"Twelve."

The nation held its breath. There was so much riding on this shot. Nothing could bring back those on *Titan*, those who'd died, but there was still the women to save.

"Eight."

"Seven."

"Six."

"Five."

The great flames began to show beneath the great bird's tail.

"Four."

"Three."

"Two."

"One."

Ponderously, majestically, reluctantly, *Atlantis*, pushed by prayer, powered by hope, lifted its great mass from the sandy soil of Florida and was on her way to rescue a group of very shaken people.

"Ladies and gentlemen, this is Ken Donovan speaking to you from the Kennedy Space Center in Florida where it appears we have a successful launch. The USS *Atlantis* which you see now on your television screen is about to attempt a rescue of nineteen women and children who are currently in their lifeboat in the sky, the European Space Agency's *Spacelab VII*.

"*Atlantis* carries a crew of four on this launch. In addition to the spacecraft commander and pilot, General Wofford Connolly and Colonel Theodore Kite, two medic astronauts are along to tend to any survivors of the *Titan* disaster."

Princess Constance of Luxembourg was angry and upset.

"Why won't they tell us?" she demanded of the *Spacelab* commander. "Do they think we're unable to . . . to handle it?"

"Do they think waiting is better?" put in Mary Fittipaldi in support of the Princess.

Stafford shook his head.

"The decision's not mine," he said as he'd told them before. I don't know any more than I've already told you. They overshot the runway and there was a severe problem. There *are* survivors."

"Who?" someone else called out. "The very fact that they put it that way tells us that there were . . . casualties." It was obviously difficult for her to get the word out. It sounded so dire, so terribly final.

"My ex-wife's aboard," Stafford said. "The mother of my child. I'm concerned, too."

"There's nothing he can do," Mame Gill pointed out. "Let's show some guts up here!"

Stafford wondered what he would have done without Mame. She was incredible. Between her and the royal lady of Luxembourg, he'd been able to maintain a reasonable degree of control in a situation without precedent or ready solution.

"Thanks," he said quietly to her.

She smiled. It was a tough little smile. Behind it he could see clearly her own worry.

"*Spacelab*, this is Houston," came the voice of Astronaut Robin Barker, Cap-Com for the *Atlantis* rescue flight.

"*Spacelab* here," Stafford responded.

"We have outstanding news for you folks," came Robin Barker's Arkansas twang. "We've just launched *Atlantis* and she's going for rendezvous."

"Jolly good, Houston."

There was little restraint aboard *Spacelab*. Tears, prayers, cheers were the order of the day. There was no further point in restraining them.

"Stand by for further instructions."

"Thank you, ma'am," he responded.

The mission was nominal. Two of the rescued passengers passed out from the excitement, but, generally speaking, all went well as *Atlantis* gently scooped *Spacelab* into her cargo bay.

"We have retrieved our egg," General Connolly called in and with a bit of satisfaction showing in his deep baritone voice. "And it doesn't appear to have been broken at all. Not a crack!"

"Outstanding," came the reply from the ground.

* * *

When *Atlantis* made a perfect landing at Edwards Air Force Base, the Vice President of the United States was standing by. Next to him stood two bandaged, somewhat worse-for-wear astronauts who had brought *Titan* in the day before.

There were no bands. There was little bunting. But there was great joy. And at the same time there was deep concern, for it was at that moment that the wives and other survivors of *Titan* were told of the fate of their loved ones who had gone in on the stricken spacecraft. Of the twenty-nine persons who rode *Titan* to its final resting point in Guadalajara, thirteen had survived, eleven passengers and two crew members.

Survivors were, besides the two pilots, Ambassador Burton, commentator William Waddell, Senator Leon Gill, magazine publisher Jackson Destin, young Prince Ahmed of Saudi Arabia, Nicolas Liopus of Liopus Shipping, Carl Fittipaldi, Ben Polikov, Benton Sprigg, retired yachtsman, Claude R. Meakin, Speaker of the House, and reporter Seymour Ward of the *Detroit Free Press*.

"How do you feel?" a pool of television reporter asked Mame Gill as she was being shepherded away to her husband's side.

Mame stopped and faced her questioner.

"How do you suppose?" she countered. "I'm relieved to be alive, heartbroken for those who've sustained such . . . devastating losses. I'm concerned about my husband and all the others who were injured physically and emotionally."

"Is it worth it, Mrs. Gill? With a husband formerly in space and a son who has been accepted into the program, do you feel it's all worth the expense, the danger?"

"Is anything worth it?" she came back quickly, taking the newsperson by surprise.

"Well . . . if you're ask—"

"Is it?" Mame insisted, interrupting.

"I don't know."

"Well, I do. There are risks. There are expenses. But there's no risk and no expense great enough to keep people from daring, from trying new things, from blazing new trails. Along with the gift of life, the Lord's put something else in us all—something that must be served."

"And what's that?"

Mame Gill didn't hesitate.

"Curiosity! Wonder! The urge to go where no one's ever gone before. That's what humanity's all about!"

EPILOGUE

It was over.

Both elements were back on solid ground. All those fated to make it had been returned more or less intact to the world of human beings.

It would be written about in the history books, rehashed endlessly on television specials, in feature articles printed in magazines and newspapers. It was real—terrifyingly so. It had taken place—the whole frightening business.

The networks, with a sense of relief, returned to their regular commercial programs. The soaps rolled on, uninterrupted. The full NASA investigative teams had already been dispatched to Mexico, swarming all over the demolished spacecraft. Medical personnel, American and Mexican, were focusing their collective talents on those who'd been injured in the unscheduled misadventure. The NASA and GSA accountants would be pouring over the bills for months. The nation would get back to business as usual. Sobered somewhat by the specter of failure, Americans could clearly see the great white bird, burned and broken, still floodlit on a foreign field.

* * *

It was a cocktail lounge on the shore of the vast Chesapeake Bay, a few miles south of Annapolis, on the opposite shore. It was, like so many such places, the new, plastic-coated reality slapped on over the old—a converted, expanded house with a gimmicky, cosmetic front. Somehow it spoke eloquently of the bankruptcy of a spent culture, a nearly used up world.

The cigarette smoke made elaborate arabesques in the air, syncopating strangely with the funky music played inside. There was empty laughter, the shuffle of dancing feet, the ten thousandth replay of the day's triumphs and tragedies on the TV over the bar.

"You planning on using that extra horn in the next set?" asked the tall, broad-shouldered patron. He was speaking to the brass man of the group taking a break on the bandstand. It was obvious they knew each other.

"No, why?"

"Like to use it."

"Want to sit in on the next set?"

"No. Use it outside."

"Outside?"

"Just want to blow."

"You and the crabs?"

"Something like that."

The musician shrugged. "Whatever turns you on."

"Okay?"

"Be my guest." The horn's owner handed the tall man the battered case.

The petitioner mumbled his thanks and took the profered case in his hands. Opening it, he took out the venerable cornet. It felt good—a decent, well-balanced old horn, battered, much used.

He threaded his way through the crowd.

It was good to be outside, to savor the fresh, if somewhat heavy air of a spring night. He filled his lungs several times, standing in deep shadow just outside the door, the one leading to the rickety dock to which patrons now and then were invited to tie their boats. There were no boats tethered on that particular night.

A full moon watched him. The damned thing looked as if it were grinning, a kind of mocking survivor's exultation.

Deliberately, still grasping the horn, the tall man strode down the old dock. He took the long, easy strides of a military man, practiced in the disciplined art of moving effortlessly, evenly, from place to place.

On regular days, whenever duty called, he was a member of the United States Marine Corps Band. Tonight he was just another civilian. He'd consumed a couple too many drinks, inhaled too much tobacco smoke, heard too much bullshit. He was bloated, sated, depressed. Was it the whisky or what he'd witnessed on TV? It was difficult to tell, to discern who was truly responsible for what.

He reached the end of the dock.

Up and down the bay, lights blinked on and off, guardians helping wayfaring mariners find their way. He could pick up the lights of a freighter moving majestically up the bay, a whole complex of brilliant lights, on her way to Baltimore or through the C&D Canal to Philly or beyond. He could hear the water lapping at the slimy pilings beneath his feet.

"Just like every other night, huh?" he muttered to no one in particular. There wasn't a soul in sight.

He raised the borrowed cornet to his lips and thought of the terrible vision he'd just watched on the tube for at least the tenth time. Mexican newscameramen had managed to capture the tumbling, blazing terror of *Titan's*

228

crash landing. It seemed such a terrible desecration of the bird he'd so admired in Florida just under forty-eight hours ago.

He pursed his lips and found the mouthpiece.

He played a familiar hymn—a traditional one. The notes were crisp and clear as they echoed out over the bay's brackish waters. He played magnificently.

The trumpeter was not fully aware, even as he played, that he had company. There was no way he could have seen them. There were no physical presences there with him on the deserted dock. Nonetheless, he was surrounded by dozens of them. United in some strange spiritual way, he played for Sager and Langenberg, clinging closely together that night in Houston. Battered mortal flesh had found solace in its complementary likeness. They were with him.

Tied to him were the Gills, the whole family reunited in a Houston hotel room. They were with the Fittipaldis, too, in Mexico where Mary patiently waited for her husband to either die or return to life and consciousness. There was the youthful Saudi Prince who'd lost his father before his very eyes and who'd assumed manhood at the same terrible moment. There was the old yachtsman, Sprigg, wondering still about the irony that had preserved him while other, younger men perished. There was the novelist, Polikov, trying to find a way to tell the wild tale he'd just been spared to write.

All of these were with the trumpeter on the moldering dock.

There were also the dead: Fisher, Pepper, the Prince of Saudi Arabia, and the Prince of Luxembourg. There was the angry ghost of the rock singer, Bieser, and the uneasy spirit of David Locke.

There were others, too—some of those who hadn't

229

made the final flight of *Titan* but who were somehow tied to it, deeply, intimately involved. At the Johnson Space Center, at that very moment, a hardbitten Mission Director, almost without knowing why, closing the book on months, days of work, uttered a prayer of thanksgiving that some had made it. In Washington, less than a hundred miles from where the trumpeter played, the President of the United States gazed out at the Rose Garden, flooded with artificial light, thinking of those who had died on *Titan*. On a plane bound for Europe, flying very close to the grave of an earlier technological marvel, the Princess of Luxembourg mourned her valiant prince, inexplicably hearing the sound of the ancient hymn in her imagination.

As the trumpeter explored the venerable melody about drawing nearer to the Godhead, each realized in his or her own place, his or her own way, that humanity is in transit toward the stars. All realized, too, through the harrowing experience they'd undergone together, that there was something yet in human beings, something within the puny human psyche that's even more formidable, more vital for the voyage to other systems than the incredible machines they devise and drive.

That was the nature of all that had taken place.

The music echoed clearly, sweetly over the water.

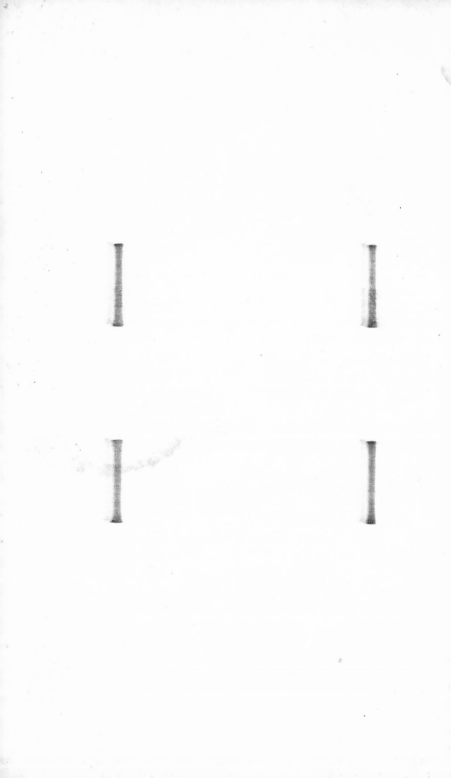